# ABOUT THIS BOOK

*Every town has stories of its past, and Havenwood Falls is no different. And when the town's residents include a variety of supernatural creatures, those historical tales often become Legends. This is but one . . .*

With the world laid out before him, Marcus St. James enjoyed the many fruits of society, none more so than the women who fell at his feet and lifted their skirts. A few whispered promises and he could have whichever beauty caught his eye. Until the night he led a young gypsy woman into the alleyway, where more than just heated kisses were exchanged.

Knocked unconscious, Marcus awakens to find his companion dead in his arms, her blood screaming for justice. Before he can uncover the truth, her family arrives—hellbent on punishing the person who murdered their kin. Ignoring his pleas of innocence, they curse him to an existence as a blood drinker.

In the wake of death, a new purpose is born, transforming Marcus into a monster. Driven by his thirst for vengeance, he focuses on hunting down the gypsies who destroyed his life. But when an innocent girl finds her way into his fortress, Marcus must decide what the true curse is: a life filled with blood and damnation or one void of love and hope. He'll discover one lasting truth—love can soften even the hardest of hearts. And can also stoke the fires of retribution.

# LEGENDS OF HAVENWOOD FALLS BOOKS

*Lost in Time* by Tish Thawer

*Dawn of the Witch Hunters* by Morgan Wylie

*Redemption's End* by Eric R. Asher

*Trapped Within a Wish* by Brynn Myers

*Blood and Damnation* by Belinda Boring

*Fated Beginnings* by E.J. Fechenda

*Emeline* by Katie M. John

*Released From a Curse* by Brynn Myers

*A Pack of Lies* by Kallie Ross

*Kiss the Ashes* by Desiree Lafawn

*Hidden Truths* by Colleen Nye

*Wrath and Retribution* by Belinda Boring

*Changing Fate* by Char Webster

*Rise of the Witch Hunters* by Morgan Wylie

*The Drowning Bride* by Seven Jane

Also try the main Havenwood Falls series; the YA line, Havenwood Falls High; the darker, sexier side of town, Havenwood Falls Sin & Silk; and the local supernatural college, Sun & Moon Academy.

Stay up to date at www.HavenwoodFalls.com

# ALSO BY BELINDA BORING

# BLOOD AND DAMNATION

## A LEGENDS OF HAVENWOOD FALLS NOVELLA

### BELINDA BORING

*To my sweet little Odie,*
*If my love alone could've kept you here, you would've lived forever.*

*To Lin-Manuel Miranda,*
*Thank you for being such an inspiration!*

# CHAPTER 1

1868

*B*lood.

It was everywhere.

There wasn't a place I could lay my hand that didn't come back covered. As I lifted my fingers to my brow, the fading sun caused the redness of the liquid to take on an even more sinister hue.

*As if being bathed in blood could get more sinister,* I chuckled silently.

There really wasn't anything funny about the situation, but for the life of me, I couldn't stop the wave of hysteria that threatened to overcome my sensibilities. It started somewhere in the base of my chest and rose with such force that to ignore it, to stifle it, would cause more pain than it was worth.

So I let it out.

Ripples of laughter echoed in my ears— sounding completely foreign and unhinged.

I shuddered to think what would happen should someone stumble by and find us like this. I imagined I would look like a madman sitting in the middle of a dirty, rat-infested alley, quietly cradling the lifeless body of a woman in his arms.

They may have witnessed the precise moment her heart stopped— the last of her lifeblood trickling slowly from her wounds.

I knew I looked disheveled, my clothes caked with blood that was already beginning to dry, my exposed skin smeared with the sticky gore. I also knew that people would not stop to ask questions. Instead, they would run screaming for the authorities.

Sounds slowly filtered back into my awareness, and the abrupt slap of reality returned me to my senses. My bloodstained hands roughly smoothed over fine black hair as if to comfort her in death.

*My victim*, I thought without hesitation.

I had somehow done this. Bile bubbled up into my mouth while I observed my gruesome surroundings, the bitter scent of copper made me gag, and numbness spread through me, shock wrapping its icy fingers around my heart.

I turned the woman's face so her lifeless eyes stared back at me, as if in death she continued to accuse me. Her name had been Primrose, or was it simply Rosa? Letting out a hasty breath, I cursed my stupidity for not remembering her name.

Whoever she was, she had been beautiful, her skin still holding a slight warmth from being held so close.

She'd caught my eye earlier in the evening as I strolled through the crowds attending the annual town fair. With her long raven-colored tresses and green twinkling eyes, I'd spent the better half of the evening exchanging glances and sensual flirtations.

London gossiped about my "rakish" ways. I had a useful talent of layering my seductive charms on so thick that it always guaranteed me getting what I wanted—whoever I wanted. My goal was that before the night was over, she'd be beneath me, writhing as I drew out every ounce of pleasure within her.

She'd responded so freely to my suggestions that it wasn't long before she'd led me to this very alley, secluded from prying eyes. I'd immediately pressed her up against the wall as my mouth devoured hers.

Her eagerness had stoked a fire in me. Gone was the frigidity I often met from my own fellow countrywomen, and my urgency was met with her own brand of fire.

With each caress, each flick of her tongue, she sent me careening out of control. When she'd softly moaned over my touching her covered breast, I'd instinctively deepened our passionate kiss.

She'd tasted of mead and sunshine.

Even now, the thought of that fevered kiss made my mouth water.

She'd felt so good and responded so well to my attentions that I'd lost track of time. One moment she was racing toward release and the next she was lying in my arms.

Dead.

I frowned, my mind desperately trying to piece the events together, but all I could sense was an oppressive fog—one that was unwilling to succumb to my frantic probing.

Something had happened, but still it remained elusive.

Shock wouldn't hold it from me forever.

Moments passed, and more sounds filled the night air.

"They'll discover us soon," I murmured, still unable to do anything but stare down at the woman who had previously set my entire body aflame.

My skin pebbled from the chill now settling over me. The sweat clinging to my once pristine shirt caused a slight tremble to begin.

Where was my coat?

My hands slowly released her, and that's when I discovered I'd taken it off to cover Rosa.

Primrose?

The body.

Muscles groaned from suddenly being forced to move, and I gingerly pushed the weight from my lap, careful to not disturb the woman further. This caused another chuckle to erupt.

The time for gentleness and consideration had passed with her last breath, but still I couldn't bring myself to think of her as dead. It felt wiser for my dwindling sanity to consider her asleep, and as if to prove that point, I leaned over one more time and tentatively laid my lips to her cool forehead for one last kiss.

My lips came back wet, no doubt glistening from her blood.

That was all the truth and reality I needed.

As my resolve snapped, I toppled to the side and began violently heaving.

"Dear God," I groaned, too weak to wipe at my mouth.

The feeble contents of my stomach mingled with the drying pool of blood as if taunting me, forming a macabre mixture.

The smells of the alley—the smell of her—assaulted my senses again, driving me to purge my stomach until all that was left was a repeated gag.

I gasped for air, my chest struggling to drag in enough oxygen to compensate for the violence. My stomach screamed from my muscles being roughly contracted.

It took everything I had to stand, staggering slightly as the world began to spin. Unable to take my eyes away from the body, I suddenly realized that I'd lingered too long.

With the alley open at both ends, a channel between two streets, it was only a matter of time before someone else would seek to use it. I had to flee. I couldn't be found here . . . not like this.

I'd made it a mere two steps before a hysterical shriek pierced the air.

Panic blasted through me as the scream evolved into guttural sobbing, revealing two strangers. One of the women threw herself to the ground and scooped Primrose up into her arms, pinning the now stiff body to her chest. Tears cascaded down her wrinkled cheeks.

Words flew out of the older woman's mouth in short spurts of some foreign language, one that sounded familiar. She wore a haunted expression, her hands frantically searching over the person I assumed was someone she knew and loved.

She was feeling for the fatal wound.

I stood transfixed, held tightly by the women's grief. Chivalry screamed for me to go comfort her, but even I knew how badly this appeared. Her loved one was dead and there I stood—smeared with her blood.

The other woman, much younger in appearance, maybe a sister or cousin, finally reached the spot of despair and flung her arms around the rocking figure. She added her sobs to the melee, and something within me jolted.

I shouldn't be watching this. This was too private, too intimate, and it wasn't for me to witness.

My traitorous foot crunched on discarded litter as I took a step away. The movement caused the air to suddenly silence as two pairs of tear-filled eyes snapped on me.

Anguished.

Wretched.

Furious.

Frozen by the honesty I couldn't ignore, I willed myself to move, to break contact with the piercing gazes that scrutinized me. It wasn't difficult to read the judgment filling their faces. They took everything in—my appearance, the blood, what I assumed was my guilt-stricken expression.

The younger woman gasped as she made the sign of the cross, her hands trembling with strong emotion. Even though she was at a distance, the word *mulo* reached my ears.

Death.

That word. I knew it. It meant death.

Pieces clicked together as my brief lover's face flashed through my mind. Primrose had been my escort for the evening. I would've recognized her heritage, had I not been so fixated on bedding her.

Guilt. Waves of guilt pulsed through my veins as memories finally surfaced.

The spell that held me broke, and without thinking, I stepped forward, moving toward the women with my hands outstretched in a sign of submission. There was no denying my sense of survival begged me to run, but honor compelled me to stay. There were explanations to be made, questions to be answered, and somewhere amongst the emotions churning thickly in the air, I hoped to uncover some of my own.

Evidence be damned. I couldn't have done this. My lust ran toward the flesh and losing myself between a pair of willingly spread legs. It wasn't in death, murder, and violence.

It was with these thoughts that my confidence slowly strengthened. Romani people were often present on my family's estate when I was growing up. I'd spent many a childhood summer running and playing with the children of different traveling families, so dealing with the two women wouldn't pose too difficult a problem.

"Hello." My voice croaked from being unused.

Angry stares answered. Neither woman spoke, which caused me to stop mid-step.

*Perhaps I'd underestimated the situation. How could this be resolved if they refused to acknowledge me?*

I did the only thing I knew to do—I tilted my head forward in a respectful bow. We English prided ourselves on having impeccable manners.

With a scratchy throat and my mouth feeling as though I was trying to swallow fireplace ash, I tried again. For a brief second, I wished I had a tankard of mead, anything that would help so I could make this speech and leave.

I took in a deep breath, and thankfully my voice didn't hold the weakness from before. I sounded strong, diplomatic, trustworthy even.

"My name is Marcus. Lord Marcus St. James of Smithersby Field . . ."

A cold tone interrupted my friendly introduction.

"We know who you are." It was the older woman, the grandmother, if I'd judged correctly, who spoke. She then punctuated her statement with a sharp noise as she spat on the ground angrily.

"We know exactly who you are. *Chor*."

My brow crinkled as I hurriedly tried to translate the foreign word. Something tugged at a distant memory. I was sure I'd heard it before, but the stress of the evening was causing me to draw an annoying blank.

"I'm sorry. I don't know what that word means," I mumbled in response.

Again, the woman interrupted.

"*CHOR*." The word rang out with a blistering force as her finger shot out, pointing straight at me. Accusation and hatred exploded across her face.

There was no withstanding the vehemence of her verbal attack. Stuttering, struggling to find a way to placate her, all I could do was stand there—speechless. For the life of me, I had no idea what she was saying.

"She's calling you a thief," the grief-stricken voice of the younger female revealed. She must've been a few years older than Primrose.

"I assure you, I am no thief. Allow me to say again . . . my name is Marcus St. James. Believe me, there's an explanation for this. This is not what it seems."

"It matters not what your name is. It's your actions that label you a thief. You stand there covered in the blood of our beloved, hoping to slip away into the night after stealing the life of sweet Primrose. You are a thief, a black-hearted stealer of innocence."

"Please, let me continue." I took another step forward. "I didn't do this. I didn't kill her. I'm not quite sure what happened. One moment we were becoming . . . *acquainted*, and then she was dead."

The moment it passed through my lips, I knew how dubious and feeble my explanation sounded. Even the most uneducated of commoners could poke a hole through it with enough certainty to convict and then hang me.

"What do you mean *acquainted*?" The question thundered brashly in the alley.

My face flushed, and I tried loosening the tightness of my shirt collar, only to find blood flaking away when I pulled my fingers back. The small pieces fluttered to the ground, some snagging the thigh of my trousers. Repulsed, I jerked violently as I tried to brush them away.

Some would say it was a compelling act of guilt—the killer unable to face the truths of his sins.

Everywhere I looked, I saw blood. *Her* blood. In some places it was so thick, it caused my clothing to stick and dry to my skin.

I gagged again, quickly covering my mouth. This wasn't a moment to show weakness, but there was no helping it. With each passing breath, my hope of escaping this nightmare grew dimmer.

"What do you mean *acquainted*?" the woman repeated. "Do you mean to stand there and say that not only did you murder my sister, but you also corrupted her with your debauched and vile ways?" Her gaze narrowed on me as if she'd already judged and condemned me.

Images from earlier returned to invade my mind.

Primrose squirming against me, her hand rubbing hard against my erection. Based on her nymph-like response, she'd definitely been corrupted, but not by me.

If there was even an inkling of possibility that they'd believe me, I would tell that to her family. I would give them a quick education on how very *unvirtuous* their precious Primrose was.

The older woman drew herself up slowly, finally coming to a stand. She'd been quietly rocking back and forth with the deceased as she watched the interaction between her kinswoman and me. She was small, as women went, the years beginning to hunch her over with a stoop. I would've sworn that as she stood there, vengeance blazing in her eyes, she grew in stature—rivaling my own height.

"*Chor!*" she accused. As she stepped around the body she'd lovingly been holding, an energy began to fill the space around them. Somewhere in the distance, I heard dogs howling as thunder shook the air. Something was stirring, and it felt as though its focal point was solely on me.

The words were coming thick and fast as the woman launched into a rhythmic speech that was occasionally broken up by her quick gasps for breath. She droned on and on for what seemed like a lifetime.

I was able to pick out the occasional word, but what I heard next chilled me to the core.

*Bibaxt.* Bad luck.

*Marime.* Outcast.

*Naswalemos.* Sickness.

*Strazhno.* Danger.

*Amria.* Curse.

That word hit me the hardest. She was cursing me, and as I propelled myself forward to stop her, a pain like nothing I had *ever* experienced drove me abruptly to my knees with a demonic roar of agony.

Fire blazed through my veins, heating then boiling my blood until I was positive my insides were liquefying. Sweat dripped from every pore as my body trembled with vicious convulsions that threatened to render me insane.

Now writhing on the floor, words failed me.

All I could see—feel—was excruciating pain.

Deep within my chest a humming began, the sensation causing my heart to beat erratically. All I wanted to do was beg for death as I felt something inside me explode. Whether from mercy or approaching unconsciousness, the pain began to fade as everything dulled. My vision darkened.

I wept with relief. As I curled up into a ball so I could welcome oblivion like a long-lost friend, a single word reached out and branded my soul.

*Shilmulo.*

A small shard of alarm pierced me the moment I recognized it, but I was without hope, the world finally crashing around me.

*Shilmulo.*

Vampire.

# CHAPTER 2

## 10 YEARS LATER

"*E*nter."

Annoyance flickered through me at the interruption. A new lead about the band of gypsies who'd cursed me to this blasted existence had surfaced, but instead of leaving to pursue it, I was stuck here, collecting a debt.

With heightened senses, I could hear her lurking outside the door as if trying to will her feet to move. This lack of spine was something I wouldn't tolerate once she became mine to do with as I pleased. Cowardice was an ugly trait—especially for a woman of her breeding.

Pity it hadn't stopped her father from being a squandering fool who believed I would show mercy and forgive his mismanagement of funds.

Hesitation seemed to still delay her in obeying my command, and my annoyance was quickly evolving into impatient anger. I had a reputation for crushing those who thought they could keep me waiting.

She wasn't the one controlling this meeting. She was merely property exchanging ownership—from the keeping of her father to mine.

"I won't ask again," I called out, knowing full well she heard me. My voice was one no one could ignore without paying the price for it.

There was a microscopic part of me that was impressed her hesitancy was because of fear and not because she was inherently rebellious. She knew who I was.

I was the fearsome Marcus St. James.

A monster.

Cruelty personified.

And unfortunately for her, her newly betrothed.

Her heart picked up its pace, that telltale sign she'd finally made the decision to act. She may be terrified of me, but she had a deep, abiding love for her father, and it was that devotion that turned the door knob.

Perhaps she still doubted that her father meant to force her to marry me. We hadn't officially met, although I'd sensed her hiding in the shadows when I'd attended her father's request that I become his financial benefactor. Her family was facing utter destitution, and he had approached me out of desperation.

I wasn't ashamed to admit I had also overheard part of the discussion between them when he broke the news of the conditions. I had no real need for money or a wife, but I saw the sense in having a blood source readily available. If anything, she was at least good for that.

"But, Father!" she'd cried, the sound of her heart breaking ringing out. "His heart is ugly . . . blackened . . . cruel. Surely, you've heard the town gossip? How can you ask this of me?"

I heard the tears in her voice, but they did nothing to move me toward empathy. Let her believe I was guilty of the foul acts I was often accused of. Her opinion meant nothing.

I could've been the very Devil himself, but she was a woman, and they had no say in the affairs of men.

Catriona finally stood, shuddering, in the doorway. Her gaze scanned the room, no doubt looking for me, but I remained hidden. Let her panic. It would teach her not to keep me waiting in the future.

"Girl, this will be the last time I repeat myself. You are to obey my every word without qualm." My voice, harsh and filled with bitterness, drew her attention in my direction.

Catriona closed her eyes and absently crossed herself before stepping completely into the room, closing the door behind her. She kept her eyes to the ground, losing what little bravery she'd somehow managed to muster.

I let out an amused chuckle.

"God won't help you. You would be wise to abandon whatever faith you cling to. He cares not for his supposed children." It was a lesson I was all too familiar with. A decade ago I had reached out—begged with all the sincerity my young, naïve heart could rally for His intercession and benevolence—only to find silence and betrayal.

Judging from her expression, the room was nothing like she'd thought it would be. She no doubt expected to find opulence and extreme finery, with my entire wealth on extravagant display. Without thinking, she raised her eyes, her mouth opening in surprise as she drank in our surroundings.

I had the room decorated for this precise reason. I loathed meeting the expectations of others. I had quickly realized the power that came from allowing others to underestimate me. It gave me the upper hand in every situation—throwing each person off their game and leaving them at my whim.

The room was definitely beautiful and unbelievably simple in its decorations. Floor-to-ceiling bookcases flanked the room on two of the four walls, and I saw the instant she fought the urge to run to the impressive library and see what treasures were displayed. The comfortable chairs and settees were strategically placed because it was the room I most used for quiet solitude. Elegant crafted lamps placed on side tables were positioned to offer the best light.

This room was my sanctuary. Very few had been granted entrance.

Silently, I watched as she turned around, momentarily transfixed. Her gaze was drawn to the portrait hanging on the wall next to the door she'd just come through.

Each brush stroke, each choice of vibrant color presented the image of a man who had no problem dominating those beneath him. The artist had been able to capture the strength of his subject, a power and authority that filled the room by the mere presence of the painting. It reflected a man who could command armies, yet held a glimmer of something else—a trace of humor and mirth in the way the eyes seemed to twinkle and the gentle lifting of the lips into a smile.

My lips.

My eyes.

Or should I say, the person I should've been, had I not been in that damned alley all those years ago. I had been tempted to smash the portrait into pieces, to set it aflame until all that remained were ashes, but oddly enough, it comforted me. At least this way, that version of me still existed.

Looking at the small brass placard at the base of the frame, Catriona reached out, letting out a gasp when she recognized the name.

*Marcus St. James.*

"Do you like what you see?" I teased, reminding her I was still in the room, and her focus on my portrait hadn't gone unnoticed. Let her fall in love with the illusion. Let her find peace in her fate.

My voice held a strange softness. She raised her hands slowly, rubbing the sides of her arms as though she was suddenly cold.

"I do. It's hard not to. This man is definitely attractive, and there's something mesmerizing about the way he presents himself," she uttered, unable to drag her gaze away from the image in front of her.

"Would he be a man you could fall in love with?" My brows furrowed. Why the hell did I care what she thought?

"I hardly think that's an appropriate question, sir."

"Answer the question." The gentleness of the moment was shattered by the ruthless command I barked out. "And don't presume to lie to me, Catriona." Her name rolled off my tongue with ease. "I've a way of always finding out the truth, and heaven help the fool who thinks they can deceive me."

Raised goose bumps danced across her skin, causing her to tremble slightly. Swallowing nervously, she answered. "Yes. Yes, I think this is a man I could fall in love with."

She let out a soft sigh, realizing that such romantic hope was folly, because the man she was to marry wasn't the image before her but the monster behind her.

"Will you not turn and address your betrothed . . . your *beloved*?" The last word was spat out with such vehemence and scorn that it caused her to jump from its force.

She slowly turned. Her confused expression elicited another chuckle from me.

I cleared my throat, a reminder that whatever she had fantasized about meeting her future husband had been in vain. She wasn't here for loving gestures and thoughtful acts.

"How do I address you, sir, if you won't show yourself?" Try as she might, she wasn't quite able to hide the curt frustration in her voice.

"Are you sure you are ready to come face to face with me? Have you fortified your delicate sensibilities? You are, after all, about to meet the Beast of Smithersby Field. Are you not scared, trembling in your corset?" I all but mocked her.

Raising her right hand to eye level, she revealed the unsteady tremble that had come over her. "As you can see, I am afraid, and wish the introduction over. If you are so concerned for my *sensibilities*, as you put it, please reveal yourself and let us speak freely. I assume there is much to discuss."

I stepped out from the curtains. I didn't bother withholding my grin as another gasp escaped through her lips.

A beast I may be, but I also knew the effect I held over the weaker sex. It was encouraging to see that I could use my physique and appearance to weaken her knees, so to speak.

I stood at almost six foot one and had been described as the epitome of masculine perfection. I could see she agreed with that sentiment as she all but licked her lips. I had inherited my father's strong face, with a defined jawline and a cleft in my chin that many females had stroked with soft fingertips.

We also shared the same hair color, that of the darkest black oil, but unlike my father, I didn't tie it back with a ribbon like most men of the time did. I'd grown accustomed to letting it hang loose.

It was my piercing blue eyes, however, that many confided bored deep down into their souls, digging about for whatever secrets they kept hidden, and I could exploit. That wasn't what made me appreciate them, though.

They were the eyes of my beloved mother—my champion. She was the one, had she lived long enough, who would've kept her only son from becoming a broken shell of his former self.

As much as I hated to admit it, my mother would've instantly approved of Catriona—pleased her darling son had found such a beautiful woman to marry. I could barely remember her voice, but something told me she would've uttered with pride how pleased she was.

I tried to view my bride-to-be as though I was peering out through my mother's eyes. What would've caught her attention? What traits would she admire? I shook away the thought softly murmuring that there were plenty of attributes I found attractive. As my gaze attempted to take in Catriona's appearance, there was no need to closely study her features—I already knew what I liked.

*Her eyes.* Philosophers shared that they were windows to the soul and everything you needed to know about the measure of a person could be found by taking a few moments to peer into their depths. Catriona's eyes terrified me because the briefest of glances—the tiniest of peeks—had felt like the strike of a match . . . an instant desire. Not in a sexual way, although there was definitely a stirring of lust within me. No, her dark eyes all but promised that should I linger . . . should I cave to temptation . . . I would find myself lost. The clarity and intelligence that stared out at me struck a chord of warning that once distracted, I would gladly walk away from the life I knew and follow her to the ends of the earth.

I didn't like that. I hated it. I refused to let another person control me or alter the path I had chosen to walk. A woman had been my downfall once before, and now this temptress stood before me—unaware of the power she held, the power that beckoned.

*Her smile,* a voice in my head gently pressed, forcing me to drop my gaze to Catriona's mouth. While her lips were only slightly curled upward, there were moments where a smile came as the result of her seeing something that pleased her. I'd caught a glimpse as she stared up at my portrait, and there was a growing need building within my chest that wanted to see it again.

This was absolute absurdity. I didn't want love. I wasn't looking for it. I was half convinced to take her by the arm, drag her back through my home, and toss her out on her behind. I didn't need a wife, or any kind of distraction, especially one that would no doubt prove to be trouble.

Yet all I could do was stare. By some miracle, I managed to keep my mouth shut, because I had the sinking suspicion that I would make myself look like a blithering buffoon or a lunatic incapable of speech.

I would need to act cautiously around her, never lowering my guard or showing any sign of softening.

I could see Catriona gathering her resolve, so she could push her fear aside.

I needed her afraid, however. If not for her, for me.

One moment I stood by the wall, and the next I was before her, grasping her hand with the intent to kiss it. Questions rose in her mind, shining out through her eyes. There was no need to ask her what they were—I had heard most of them before.

*How did I move so fast?*

*Why did I toy with her like a cat plays with a mouse?*

*Why wasn't I acting completely monstrous, instead keeping her unbalanced?*

She lowered her eyes out of habitual respect, yet the nicety of the moment vanished when I flipped over her hand and buried my mouth in her palm, nudging the soft flesh with my lips. Her skin heated when I pushed her buttons further, the tip of my tongue caressing her skin in light swirls.

Her knees buckled this time, and without thought, my arms banded around her waist, pulling her flush against my hard body. Propriety demanded she ask to be released, and truth be told, I wasn't quite sure I would honor it.

I liked how she felt.

*Damn.*

She couldn't help but shudder with pleasure as I nipped at the meat of her palm with my teeth. Whatever resistance she'd felt all but melted away as she softened against me further.

Intriguing.

I curled my finger under her chin, raising it until she was looking up into my eyes. Common sense finally took back the reins, and she tried to back away, but I refused to release her.

I should have.

I should've returned to where I'd been standing and kept the space between us until I understood the lust now bubbling up within me. It was hard to believe such a frail female could be dangerous, but I could feel her presence chipping away at my intentions.

All I had wanted was to put a greater fear in her—help her understand that the life she'd once dreamed about was gone and lost forever.

Instead, my mouth came down over hers.

It was as if the heavens opened and a chorus of angels began to sing their praises. Passion burst through me, and as inexperienced as she was, it didn't take her long to know what I expected.

As my tongue flicked out against her closed lips, she parted them willingly and actually groaned when I caught a taste of her.

Her hands moved up over my shoulders and wrapped around my neck. It sent off an alarm inside my brain—that she was taking liberties I hadn't yet granted her. I was the master here—*her* master— and she touched me as though we were consensual lovers.

We would never be lovers in that sense. Ever.

My body betrayed me, and I tugged on the back of her head, my hands fisting in her thick, silky hair. I deepened the kiss, and with it, I almost lost what remained of my sanity.

Time seemed to stand still.

Her body began to rub against me, and I felt that familiar pressure building—one that felt urgent, hot, and needy.

I moved us, pinning her against one of the bookcases. Catriona gasped as my hands found her breasts, kneading them with my fingers.

Gripping onto my shoulders, gathering fistfuls of my shirt, she dipped her head back, and the movement exposed her throat.

I exhaled sharply—instantly stopping.

Her breath now came out in heavy pants, but that wasn't what held me hostage.

My lips found her skin again, my tongue tracing the contour of her neck. It was the one spot that always controlled me, although I fought it with everything I had.

Her pulse.

Gently, I began sucking on the spot, and it caused her heart to race so fast, I could feel it against my mouth.

That was when I realized she wasn't the one in the most danger.

It was also when I began second-guessing my decision to accept her as payment. There was nothing sweet and innocent about the young woman limp with pleasure in my arms.

No, she was much, much more than that.

There was a good chance she was one of Satan's sirens—sent to tempt me to Hell with lust—the one who believed it would be her to bring me into submission.

It was that last thought that acted like a much-needed slap in the face.

Dumping her unceremoniously on the floor, I fled from the room, driven from my own sanctuary like the Black Plague had returned to claim me as its victim.

I was no one's victim—not anymore.

Never again.

# CHAPTER 3

*W*e didn't talk again until a week later.

She was already moved in, Knox having placed her in a room that was as far away from me as possible. I didn't want her entertaining any kind of illusion that she could tame me, or that she was in fact *wanted*.

She was a means to an end.

If there was one thing she could rely on from me, it would be that I was consistent.

I would *consistently* keep her at a distance.

I would *consistently* remind the annoying female I was not her knight in shining armor and there would be no happily ever after in her future.

It was the only offering I would bestow on her.

She ranked just below the discarded furniture stored away in the wing she now lived in. I felt some kind of emotion toward the antiques passed down through the generations, however.

I could at least see some functional use for them.

She'd finally spotted me passing through the kitchens quickly, having spent the past hour walking the estate. It had become my nightly routine and was one of the very few rituals that brought me any semblance of peace.

That contentment shattered as soon as I heard her shriek my name.

Truth be told, this confrontation was days overdue. Part of me had expected her to barge into each and every room in the house, searching to see where I'd been hiding.

What she didn't understand was it wasn't really hiding when you had zero intentions of spending time together in the first place.

My hands clenched by my side, and even though I willed them to relax, they simply tensed up again.

Would I ever be able to roam freely about my home again without being pestered?

"What happened?" Her voice was filled with accusation and anger.

I replied with stony silence. I didn't care how much that unsettled her.

She reached out to touch me, an unforgivable act, and stumbled back when I moved like lightning, roughly grasping her wrist with a steel-like grip.

Tears flooded her eyes at the pain.

Bending her wrist slightly, I added enough pressure to elicit another moan of pain.

Damn, the sound was like a shot of pure, unadulterated lust to my groin. As she looked up at me, her rage was replaced with undiluted fear.

Gone was any semblance of defiance. In her eyes, the *monster* was fully unleashed.

I towered over her smaller form, forcing her to cower before me.

"Don't *ever* make the mistake of touching me. You will not survive the consequences." I kept my tone cold on purpose.

"I'm sorry." Catriona cringed at the way her voice had quickly devolved from confident to whimpering. "I didn't mean to interrupt you. I just wanted to know what happened."

"What do you mean? Nothing happened." I spat the words out impatiently, releasing her wrist and brushing past her. I didn't have time for such feminine nonsense.

"But the last time we spoke . . . you and I . . . we—" She had the decency to appear humiliated about bringing up last week, and the fact that I feigned ignorance.

I knew exactly what she referred to. Memories of the kisses we'd exchanged and the way she roused the man in me still plagued me at the most inopportune times.

I whirled around, wearing what I hoped was a look of complete derision. All I could see was the ghost of her swollen lips and the breathless way her chest had heaved with passion. Each step I now took toward her caused her to retreat—as though she recognized the predator in me and that she was prey to be stalked.

I shoved her to the door, finally pressing her body against the frame with my own.

It was infuriating how perfectly we fit and how incredible she smelled as the subtle perfume of her skin infiltrated my senses.

The wind blew, rustling the leaves on the tall trees that stood proudly in the gardens. There was no one but Knox around, but I had no idea whether she'd met him yet—whether he'd deemed her worthy of his attention. I kept him busy on projects of vital importance. It wouldn't surprise me if he avoided her just as much as I did.

"There is no one to hear you scream, Catriona. No ally to protect you." Without thinking, I traced the curve of her cheek with my finger. Too soft for her own good.

"Should I be crying out for help?" she countered bravely. I could see the thread of restraint that kept her from shrinking back from my touch. *In some other lifetime . . .* it was a thought I couldn't indulge.

Loneliness could be something we held in common—separately.

She clutched the doorframe for strength.

"You think that inconsequential display of affection meant something? Did you suppose it's something you can look forward to once we're married? Or are you hoping for another taste, perhaps?" I searched her face for the answer and replied with a deep throaty laugh that flushed her cheeks with a mottled shade of red. "You did, didn't you?"

She tried to hide the hurt she was feeling and failed. It was her own fault that she'd gotten caught up in the moment and romanticized me into someone with a heart. Someone with the ability to show and enjoy passion.

"Poor fool of a girl. How about some brutal honesty since we're to be married? I took one look at you gazing at my portrait with such lovestruck eyes and felt nothing but pity for you." I reached up and pushed a lock of hair back from her face. Instead of lowering my arm, I traced the side of her face as I crooned softly into her ear. "So soft. So innocent. So horribly naïve."

Catriona tried to fight her way out of my tight embrace, but came up short because she was no match for my superior strength. Clutching the sides of her arms now, I shook her. Hard. The force caused her head to roll back and slam against the door.

My cruelty was rewarded with an unwanted twinge of guilt.

Had I truly become the very creature people accused me of being —that I often told myself I was? How had I completely lost sight of the young man I had once been before that fateful evening a decade ago?

I instantly squashed that emotion. It would only undermine the person I *had* to be in order to survive the curse.

"Let. Me. Go," she demanded through gritted teeth.

"Not until we get this foolishness of yours resolved. Consider what happened a gift, the only one you will ever receive from me. The man in that portrait is dead, and no amount of girlish charm will resurrect him. Accept that and we may be able to reside alongside each other in tentative peace. All thoughts of affection, loving gestures, sweet whispered words are fruitless. You will receive none from me. This is an arrangement that comes from the ridiculous begging of your father. The man is a fool who squandered his fortune and then expected someone to reach into their pockets and save him. Nothing in this life is free. Everything has a price, and you, Catriona, are the price for your family's pride and vanity."

Her temper rose again in her eyes. I'd besmirched her father's name directly to her face. Her hands formed into claws, and I knew she wanted to reach up and scratch my eyes out for showing such dishonor.

I grasped her arm and brutally squeezed.

"That got your attention. Learn now that I won't be ignored. When I speak, you would do well to hang on my every word as though it came from the mouth of God. I'm to be obeyed and maybe, just maybe, you will survive this farce of a life forced on both of us."

"You bastard!" She raised her hand to slap me across the face and almost connected before I wrenched it away. I'd finally found the limit to her patience and self-control.

"So you're not the submissive mouse you pretend to be. Good to know. It can be beaten out of you, if you think to push me. Don't ever think you can raise your hand to strike me. In three days, I will own you, and you'll be mine to do with as I please. Play the role of the dutiful wife well, and I may just leave you alone. Annoy me, and you'll wish you'd never stepped foot in this house. Do I make myself clear?"

Catriona refused to look at me, another rush of defiance keeping her from caving to my demands. It was as if she silently challenged me to do my worst.

Foolish. Very, very foolish. I hoped she never got to witness firsthand the extremes I had, and would go to, in order to get what I wanted.

"I asked you a question."

Resentment shone from her eyes as she met my gaze. She realized she truly was a prisoner here, that I was her warden, and that returning to her former life was a hopeless cause. Tears flowed down her cheeks as she fully understood the extent of her situation.

What she didn't know was that I was just as much a prisoner to this life as she was.

"I understand, sir."

"Good. Now go away and do something. I'm sure you have things that will occupy your time here. If you don't, talk with the maid I've hired for you, and see what she suggests. I trust we won't have to meet too often once we're married. It may serve you well to find a friend."

Catriona nodded her head, biting on her bottom lip. She wiped at her cheeks with the back of her hand, and when I finally let her move freely, she turned to retrace her steps out of the kitchen. Right before she left, with her back to me, she asked one last question.

"What about children?"

My incredulous gasp answered it.

"What makes you think I would want to bring children into this shamble of a life?"

Her mouth popped open with a gasp. I'd shocked her.

"You want no sons? No heirs?" Judging from her response, the idea was beyond anything she could understand. It was something that society drummed into us from childhood—that the greatest accomplishments a man could achieve was his ability to pass his legacy on to his children. Her gaped mouth showed she'd never met anyone who thought the idea of it a joke.

"You don't want to pass your legacy on?" The question flowed from her mouth without thought.

"You have no idea what you're asking, Catriona." I'd grown tired of the conversation and brushed her away with a hand gesture. "Go away. Your questions offend me." This would be the last warning she got.

With my hand on the doorknob to go back outside into the twilight air, I ignored the melancholy that descended across her gentle features.

Let her be sad.

Let her be disappointed.

*Welcome to the ways of the world, wife-to-be.*

*Welcome to reality.*

# CHAPTER 4

Fiddling with the last cufflink on my sleeve, I quickly glanced over my shoulder to the only person with permission to enter my bedchambers unannounced.

Phineas Knox—manservant and trusted confidant. Our relationship was a far cry from the business-driven contract I'd initiated when I first met him. Back then, he had merely been a necessary cog in the machine—someone to run my errands while I chased every rumored gypsy sighting across England and into Scotland.

It had taken me a while to call him by the correct first name. Who he was personally was inconsequential and I hadn't cared enough to learn anything about him—other than to exact his complete obedience. By chance, I'd discovered that his talents and skills lay beyond the superficial running of an estate and ensuring his master's needs were met.

Knox was a man who held great value.

He would bring me the cure on a silver platter—most likely with hands splattered with the blood of those he forced to bend to my will.

"You plan on wearing that to the ceremony?" he asked quizzically. He strode over to where I stood before the full-length mirror and began brushing along my shoulder blades—straightening the fabric of my shirt.

"Am I expected to dress up?" I retorted, checking my appearance. My linen shirt was pressed to perfection, and my black trousers held a sharp crease down the front. I didn't move as he finished his own inspection.

For all intents and purposes, to the outside world, he was my valet. When we were alone, we often continued the façade, even when there was no one to witness it.

"Honestly, Marcus?" he offered me a respectful bow and came to a stop beside me. "I anticipated finding you in your underclothing, clothes crumpled and creased from the lack of care. You've made it perfectly clear that today's formalities are simply that and that you hold no affection for the girl. I've seen you show more excitement over the prospect of inspecting new horses for your stables."

"Well, one usually dresses to impress for their wedding, Knox." I didn't bother hiding the sarcasm or smirk that danced across my lips.

My wedding.

How the hell did I allow things to get this far?

"Have you seen her yet? Did you deliver the outfit I requested she wear?"

Part of me wished I'd been a fly on the wall when he presented her with the garment I'd found stuffed in a long-forgotten storage trunk that once belonged to a dead ancestor. Insects had eaten jagged holes in the yellowed lace, thread hanging loosely from various hems. I had no idea whether it could be laundered back to its former glory, but deep down, I felt it was an appropriate representation of this whole fiasco.

She wouldn't be the blushing bride, and I wasn't the doting husband.

If it fit her, that was sufficient for me.

Knox cocked his eyebrow before nodding his response. "And she was far from . . . enthusiastic."

He'd searched for the right word—always in his role as a diplomat.

It's why I had kept him in my services for so long. He knew how to soften my edges when interacting with others.

I shrugged on the last item of my outfit he held up behind me, sliding my arms into a dark blue jacket. "How she feels is not my concern. She could always attend the ceremony wearing nothing, if that is more to her liking."

He burst into laughter. "Why does she irritate you so much? She's pleasant to look at, and I'm sure if you treated her with even a shred of civility, she would warm your bed quite nicely. Do you truly have to act like such a bastard toward her?"

"How I treat my betrothed is not your concern," I quietly warned, catching his gaze in the mirror's reflection. I all but spat out the word betrothed. The truth was, I still felt resentful this was becoming a reality.

Women were good for only a handful of things.

They were nuisances, otherwise, always getting involved in affairs that didn't involve them. One look at Catriona, and I had instantly recognized that same defiant spirit, one that would no doubt become a thorn in my side for years to come.

"I beg to differ, *friend*." He added his own weight to the word. "Surely you see that this borderlines on cruelty. Set her free and let her at least claim some semblance of contentment. Marriage to you will not be easy."

"Don't forget your place."

"How can I, when you enjoy reminding me on a daily basis?" There was no malice or resentment in his response. In fact, his grin revealed that as always, his loyalty lay with me. "Sometimes twice, if I'm a good boy."

"Have I told you how much I hate you?" I grumbled, my mind already flickering forward to what was about to happen. Marriage had once been the ideal—the expectation bequeathed on every son to carry on the family lineage. I'd abandoned all hope once I realized that life was no longer compatible with the one I was now forced to endure. "Summon her to my office."

I didn't wait for an answer.

Knox would obey, and this farce would be official within the hour. The last thought I had as I left my bedchambers was a hollow one.

I should've seized control of his estate instead. That would've at least made a hell of a lot more sense than this did.

A wife.

One more cursed achievement to add to a growing list of many.

TRUE TO HER SEX, Catriona was late, no doubt using her tardiness as one last, failed attempt at showing her defiance and reluctance to follow through with her father's deal.

I refused to pity her. She had been born a female and therefore knew this was her lot in life—to never have control over her own destiny. Unfortunately, that had been placed in my hands.

Even the local minister whom I'd overpaid an exorbitant amount to hurry along the process and abandon tradition was impatiently shifting his weight back and forth on his feet. He knew better than to try to engage me with small talk.

There was no commiserating over the weather we were experiencing. He hadn't so much as peeped about a possible donation to the parish. Instead, Father Thompson stood in his worn priestly garb and stared at the closed door—as if to will Catriona's appearance so he could then flee the house and my presence.

Finally, the doorknob jiggled, and despite my efforts to not turn and greet the person entering, I obediently glanced over, and that's when I experienced something I had long thought dead.

Speechless. I was utterly, unbelievably, uncontrollably . . . speechless.

She was positively angelic.

Despite the fact I had given her a nightmarish dress to wear, she'd somehow managed to make it look regal—her head held high. The material hung on her smaller frame, a partially ripped hem dragging across the floor behind her.

But you wouldn't have known that she noticed the pitiful garment and that it was a far cry from what she'd imagined wearing as a small girl.

That wasn't what almost brought me to my knees—what left me with an overwhelming need to run as far away from the creature now standing before me.

She was exquisite.

She was perfection.

*She is mine*, a voice whispered, claiming her instantly.

"Let's hurry this up," I growled, grinding my teeth tightly to prevent any soft-hearted platitude from escaping. "There are more important affairs to take care of."

I barely managed to drag my gaze away from Catriona's features to glare at the priest.

"Is my father not coming?" Her words came out broken, and I could sense the tears that lay barely beneath the surface. She didn't dare look about, in case it confirmed what I was about to say.

"No. This is not a celebration. I assume he is off enjoying his newfound freedom, having escaped debtors' prison." I resented the pressing urge to look at her—to comfort her. This was not part of the arrangement I'd committed to.

"Could we . . ." Her request died on her lips.

For some bizarre reason, I wanted to hear her complete it. "Could we what?" I pushed, gruffly.

"Nothing. As you said, this is strictly business, and I am merely your chattel." Catriona kept her gaze trained on the floor, patiently standing still with her hands clasped in front of her. Even in her misery, she held an ethereal quality. One might've even suggested she was fae-like.

"At last, something we agree on." Nodding to the priest, I indicated that it was time to begin. Father Thompson began droning on about marital bliss and the wonders of a man and woman joining together in the sight of God.

"Father," I corrected, reminding him that this was not the speech I had given him permission to do. Platitudes were wasted in this room.

We would never be a typical husband and wife, so there was no need for flowery poems and heartfelt vows.

Catriona would obey me, and in exchange, I would tolerate her presence in my life.

The priest coughed and cleared his throat, flipping through the small brown leather book in his hands until he found what he was looking for. With as little feeling as possible, I recited back the words that I would take Catriona Livingston as my wife—excluding any promises that I would cherish and care for her until death did us part.

Catriona's bottom lip trembled when it was her turn to pledge her fealty and devotion to me—her new monster of a husband. Her eyes didn't quite meet mine, and her fingers were white from constantly gripping her hands so tight. Silent tears fell down her cheeks—the blasted liquid somehow increasing her appeal.

Energy pulsed through me, and I ached to move. It was becoming more and more unbearable to remain in the room with her, each ticking sound of the clock wearing on my nerves.

No sooner had the priest declared our union official when Knox burst into the office. His dark hair was windswept, his eyes bright with excitement. I hadn't questioned his absence from the ceremony, because looking for him would require time I didn't want to waste.

"Yes?" I asked, already dismissing Father Thompson and Catriona. I was more interested in knowing what made Knox practically brim over with enthusiasm. "You have something."

"A lead!" he exclaimed triumphantly.

It had been months since we'd received any new information about the gypsies responsible for my curse. It had left me no choice but to learn years ago the importance of patience. Sometimes answers required a lengthy wait.

I would never rest until I found them.

"Let's go," I fired back, the thrill of the hunt already stirring within my breast. I was already halfway to the door when I noticed Knox hadn't moved, his own gaze directed to those behind me.

Catriona.

Barely remembering my manners, I spun about and bowed.

"Excuse me, wife." There was a slight mocking tone to my words. "It seems business waits for no man. I trust you can take care of yourself until we return."

She nodded, and I could almost detect a hint of relief. There would be no wedding night. "When shall I expect your return?"

I drank in one last sight of her.

"When it is time to return."

And with that, we departed—racing away into the night.

# CHAPTER 5

## FOUR MONTHS LATER

Soft footsteps approached my office door. It was the same sound I heard each evening as I sat at my desk, looking over papers. At first I had felt irritated by the disturbance, knowing that it was Catriona who lurked beyond the closed door. I could almost imagine her standing there with indecision warring across her features while she tried to decide whether or not she would knock.

Would tonight be the night that she found her courage and ventured inside? And how would I react to the interruption?

I'd like to think that I would answer consistently—with a stern and impatient retort, shooing her away like whatever it was that brought her to me was inconsequential.

On the odd occasion when she'd entered the study and found me sitting by the fire, reading one of the many books I'd collected over the years, she nervously licked her lips before asking if there was anything she could get me.

I wasn't a fool. I recognized the bravery needed to approach me. I hadn't made it easy for her since our pathetic excuse for a wedding. I'd warned her afterward that I wasn't to be disturbed and that for her own good, it would be best that we try to avoid one another.

There was no mistaking the crestfallen expression that glimmered in her eyes. Despite every attempt I'd made to keep her at arm's length, she was determined to breach the barrier I'd placed between us.

I found small trinkets throughout the house—items that she'd somehow known would please me. Countless nights I'd entered my study for solitude and there would be some type of treat. I'd even walked in to discover freshly cut flowers from the garden arranged in a crystal vase in my bedroom.

My first instinct was to hunt down my disobedient wife and rebuke her for violating the sanctuary of where I slept, but something inside me counseled that I tread carefully. For what reason I didn't know. Sure enough, the next time I passed by her in the house, the words that formed in my mouth went unspoken.

Even with all the precautions I took to not allow her closer, she was changing me with her small acts of kindness.

She still lurked outside, and as I closed my eyes, I could faintly hear the beating of her heart. I held my own breath this time and silently willed her to enter. If only to see what her reasoning was tonight.

She fascinated me.

She terrified me.

"Catriona," I called out, summoning her to come in.

The door handle jiggled slightly, and then it stopped moving. What would she do?

A few moments later, she retreated, making her way back up the hallway from where she'd come. I guess tonight wasn't a night for conquering fears.

I sat there staring at the door, but it was my thoughts that kept me from returning to my reading. I'd lost count of how many conversations I'd had with myself since that night when I'd been cursed. I tried not to think about what might've happened if I'd been far away from that alley, or better yet, had never laid eyes on Primrose. I'd allowed my lust to override common sense and had been punished for that decision ever since.

I could've been anything I wanted—anyone I wanted—because

the world had truly been mine to explore. Having been born into wealth and privilege, very few doors had been closed to me.

Yet, here I sat behind one, shut away from the world. I had what many would call a beautiful wife, a woman who appeared to at least try to bridge the distance between us.

For each small kindness she extended, I returned it with indifference. She didn't deserve such treatment. What scared me even more was the voice that had started whispering to me since I met her —that I didn't deserve such a life either.

Monster or not, I was at a crossroads. I would either need to let Catriona in or squash any hope she may have of melting the iciness in my heart.

Pushing away from my desk, I decided to seize the moment and follow her. I needed to understand what drew me to her—what made her so different that I was finding it harder and harder to resist.

Instead of going upstairs, however, the sound of Catriona's footsteps revealed she wasn't heading to her bedroom suite. Curiosity piqued my interest. She was hurrying in the opposite direction, and if I guessed right, toward the rooms reserved for Knox.

*Interesting*, I murmured beneath my breath.

Then, to my complete surprise, she briefly knocked on his door before entering. There was no waiting to be granted entrance. There was no gruff appearance of Knox—annoyed that she would dare to invade his privacy.

Anger rose sharply, followed by jealousy. How often did they meet late at night? What could they possibly have to discuss? And even though I'd shown no interest or intention of ever treating her like a true wife, there was no mistaking the word that came rushing to the forefront of my mind . . .

*Mine.*

Ready to burst through the door and catch them in the midst of their indiscretion, all logic and reason abandoned by the irritating sense of possessiveness, I abruptly stopped in my tracks when I caught the first sound of her voice.

She was crying.

Something—someone had upset her.

Reduced to spying on others in my own home, I reserved judgment for a moment and listened in, my ear close to the door. Despite the fierce pangs of mistrust I was feeling, there was one thing I did know with certainty . . . Knox had never given me a reason to doubt his loyalty. There was something else happening—another motive for Catriona to enter his room like they were friends meeting. Like she belonged there.

A muffled noise broke through her sobs.

"Why won't he let me in?" came the broken words of the woman crying like her heart was splintering into pieces. I pushed down the guilt that surfaced. I owed her nothing.

Or did I?

I could almost picture Knox standing there, unsure of how to handle someone so emotional. He'd shared that he'd had sisters growing up, but from the stories he'd confided in me over the years, he wasn't particularly close with them.

"What happened, Catriona?" he asked with compassion. It was strange hearing him speak so softly and tenderly. The only time I'd heard him talk in such a way was when he soothed a spooked horse down in the stables. He had a magic touch with animals, the creatures instantly calming under his touch and guidance. It was a trait I often envied. It was as if they could sense the beast I was . . . the predator I was cursed to be.

"I wanted to wish him good night. I remember you told me that such simple things might work in softening his attitude toward me."

*Knox had told her that? How often did she come to him?* Questions flurried around inside my head, each one left unanswered. Part of me knew I could barge in and demand the information I wanted, but it was a wiser part that urged for me to remain hidden. Sometimes the things you seek can only be revealed through being still and silent.

"And?" There was a hint of concern in that one word. I didn't blame him. I knew who I was and how others saw me. No amount of counsel had managed to tame my rough edges. I'd assumed he'd given up trying.

There was silence before she quietly answered. "I was a coward. I left before he could yell at me." There were a few more betraying sniffles. "I don't understand why he hates me so much, Knox. He doesn't even know me! Am I to be condemned to a life of misery because of my father's foolishness with money?"

The guilt had returned, and it frustrated me. I was tempted to flee back to my office where I could put more distance between this blasted woman and me. Maybe I would show her how truly cruel I could be and send her away to live in a nunnery. There she could curse my existence to her heart's content. She would at least find some semblance of peace.

"Give him time, Catriona. I told you. Marcus is not the man you assume him to be. I warned you it wouldn't be easy, but you were adamant that you could break down his walls. Remember, I told you it was a foolish waste of time."

It was interesting to hear him speak so freely about me.

"How can you sit there and defend him? Why won't you talk to him on my behalf? Tell him how lonely I've been and how much I wish to at least be friends? Food I take him, hoping that it will tempt him, is left untouched. The other day I found the freshly clipped roses I'd gathered tossed in the pile to be thrown away. It's as if he's doing this on purpose to drive me crazy!" As she uttered each word, I could hear her anger growing stronger and stronger. I didn't blame her. I would never accept such treatment myself. I wanted to not care, but that lack of sentiment felt like it was slipping through my fingers.

"Catriona, my loyalty belongs with him. He is my master, and no matter how many tears you shed, or how often your lip quivers, there's nothing I can do to change your circumstances here. You asked for my advice, and I gave it."

I bent forward and tried peeking through the large keyhole. There they both were—Catriona standing still with her arms wrapped around herself, and Knox, perched on his workbench stool, turned about so he could face her. Just as I had assumed, there was a hint of frustration at being kept from his work, but he was also staring at her with sympathy.

"So, you truly won't help me?" Tears began welling in her eyes. Catriona looked longingly at him . . . beseechingly. "I am all alone."

He slowly stood and walked over to where she stood. I expected Knox to guide her toward the door, but instead, he wrapped an arm around her shoulder for comfort. "Don't give up. If this is something you really want, then you will have to use that stubbornness I've seen in you. Fight for what you want. If at first you don't succeed, step back, re-evaluate, then try again."

Wiping her face with her fingers, Catriona slumped with resignation. "I didn't imagine it would hurt this much, Knox. I told myself that hope would be futile when it came to this marriage. I knew I was merely property exchanging hands. I didn't wish for a love-filled marriage . . . I'm not that naïve. But what harm could come from being friends? Am I really that unlikable?"

I couldn't see Knox's face. He squeezed her shoulder once more before dropping his arm. "You're asking questions I don't have the answers to, and what I do know, I can't share without betraying his confidence." Fingers raked through his ash-blond hair, a gesture I'd seen him make countless times. He was ready for the conversation to be over. He was ready to return to his work that beckoned him to finish.

Catriona let out a loud sigh. "Then I will keep trying." She gave one last glance about the room, and headed toward the door I was hiding behind. "Just tell me one last thing. Was he always like this?"

"Like what?" Knox asked over his shoulder, having already turned his back.

"Unapproachable. Cold. Indifferent."

He caught her gaze and held it. "He has good reason to be untrusting. Earn his respect, and you'll see he's not the monster you believe him to be." Having said all he intended to say, Knox returned his attention to his work, dismissing her.

I quickly stepped back to hide in the shadows, not wanting to let them know that I had been eavesdropping like a common thief. There was a strange mixture of emotions flittering about in my head.

There was pride and gratitude that Knox had kept my secrets, proving that my faith and trust in him were well placed.

There was a growing sense of apprehension that Catriona was determined to establish some kind of relationship with me—despite my many protests. But I was also impressed that she wasn't relying on her beauty or feminine wiles in seducing me. She had known immediately that such attempts would fail, and instead, tried to find ways to please me.

Watching her finally retreat in the direction of her own rooms, I stayed where I was for a moment, trying to absorb everything I'd heard.

"It's safe to come in now, Marcus."

He'd known I'd been there. Clearly I'd underestimated how observant he could be.

"I'm glad she has someone to talk to," I countered, entering his work space.

"She wants to be free to speak with you . . . her husband." He didn't bother disguising his bold smirk.

"I am her husband in name only," I retorted, completely unamused with this side of him. He was getting more and more brazen when we talked. It usually didn't bother me, unless, like now, he was not agreeing with me.

He cocked his brow, his boyish features turning hawkish. "I believe it was you that decided that, Marcus. I am but your obedient servant."

I ignored his last comment, choosing to focus on the more important issue. "You're to stop giving her advice. If she comes to you again, send her away. We don't have time for comforting a lonely female. Your focus is best placed elsewhere." I gestured to the experiments that covered his workspace. "That is why I hired you."

"Yes, master," he replied, with only a hint of contrition in his voice.

"No more," I reiterated, reinforcing that whatever alliance Catriona believed she had with Knox would be ended from this moment forth. "There is too much at stake."

I didn't wait to hear his response. He knew that what I said was law, and that whatever flights of fancy he might be entertaining by encouraging Catriona's visits would no longer be tolerated.

It didn't stop me from dwelling on it the rest of the night, though.

I didn't want her.

I didn't love her.

So why did I hate the idea of his arm around her shoulder, her turning to him for comfort so much?

# CHAPTER 6

## TWO MONTHS LATER

There was something peaceful about a quiet room where the only noise was the gentle crackling from the fireplace. Winter had descended with a vengeance on the estate, and with the colder weather came unavoidable duties to perform.

For the most part, we were ready for the long months where glistening snow covered every inch of the Suffolk countryside. I didn't allow it to hinder my true work, however. With my extended life, I braved the chilly conditions, pushing on when most men would retreat, because truth waited for no one.

One of these days I was certain I'd find the gypsies who cursed me, and if not them specifically, at least their clan. I wouldn't rest until I held their lives in my own two hands, satisfied only when they had removed their magic.

My heart screamed for vengeance, and even having the curse removed wouldn't curb my thirst for retribution. They had judged me without knowing all the facts. I would return that favor tenfold.

The leads Knox had brought to me months earlier had dwindled away into nothing, just as the fire in the hearth would do. It was part of the frustration that slowly ate away at my psyche. Every tidbit of information had to be explored, but not every morsel bore fruit.

We'd hit a dead end, and for the last few months, had heard little else.

I was itching to get out on the road and far away from the estate accounts that now demanded my attention.

*And from her*, I silently choked back, trying to ignore how easily her face surfaced in my mind. She was like a plague that decimated my hard-earned resolve. I didn't want to think about Catriona, or the way her defiance tugged at my focus.

I should be furious.

I should seek for ways to teach her a lesson, but the maddening woman didn't care. She spoke her mind whenever she managed to corner me, and I'd finally taken to avoiding areas of the house I knew she frequented.

My threats often fell on deaf ears, something Knox liked to rub in my face.

The knock at the door disrupted the peace, and I mentally prepared myself for who was on the other side.

"Go away," I called out.

The handle turned, and Knox entered, his face filled with tension. "Marcus—" he began.

I didn't bother looking up from the page I'd been reading. "She is your problem, Phineas. Whatever she's done, deal with it."

Dipping the quill in the black inkpot, I scribbled out the numbers I was tallying. The estate was in better shape than I'd assumed.

"Trust me, I've tried." His voice was filled with exasperation and annoyance. I didn't envy him. She was infuriating enough that even the pope himself would jump into the deepest ocean to escape her.

"Well, obviously not hard enough, if you're standing there expecting me to intervene." I placed the quill on the desk and folded my arms across my chest as I sat back in the chair. "Let me guess. She wishes to go to London for some pretty trinket?"

The affairs of women were lost on me. What they wanted was beneath my attention.

Knox cocked his eyebrow at me, unimpressed. "Do you really

think that little of me? That I would need to come have you hold my hand over something so trivial?"

He was right. While I hadn't told him such, his patience with dealing with all the unpleasantness that infiltrated my life was commendable.

"I'm sorry, my friend." I bowed my head respectfully. I'd interrupted him before even giving him the chance to explain. "What's the matter?"

"She's found him."

My gaze narrowed on him. I'd heard no horses approaching the house, no cloaked riders delivering messages. There was only one *she* he could've been referring to.

And by found him . . .

The chair I'd been sitting on teetered close to tipping from the force of my standing. Estate business came to an abrupt end as I stormed toward the door.

"How did she find him? What the hell have you been doing?" I didn't wait for him to catch up as I continued to rant over my shoulder. "How difficult is it to keep track of one pesky female?"

He was wise to not answer, choosing instead to hurry behind me as I headed toward the one place in the entire house Catriona had no business venturing.

Angry footsteps resounded in the air as we raced down stone steps to the rooms I'd affectionately dubbed my dungeons. The only people, besides Knox and myself, who saw the inside of said rooms were those unlucky enough to cross me.

Right now, that title was reserved for one man, and one man alone —my only souvenir from my search months ago.

I heard her before I saw her—Catriona's voice growing louder and louder on my approach.

"Marcus," Knox warned, calling out right as I put my hand against the door and pushed. "Remember who she is."

"She's a nuisance and a thorn in my damn side," I countered angrily, my response the only alert to those in the room.

Catriona jumped as guilt skated across her features. She knew she'd been caught and that there would be hell to pay, but that didn't stop her from then positioning herself in front of the chained man in the center of the cell. Her arms spread out as if to protect him somehow from more harm.

Little did she know how close she came to feeling the full weight of my wrath.

"You are a monster!" she screamed, fire blazing in her eyes. "How long has this man been here? Why do you have him chained like some animal?" When she couldn't get the response she wanted from me, she turned to Knox. "Free this man now!" Catriona punctuated her demand by pointing at the motionless form on the chair.

Knox simply stood there with his hands behind his back. He wasn't there to jump to her every command. He knew better than to listen to anyone but me. While we enjoyed a close relationship, Phineas never forgot who his master was.

"So, you are a coward, too!" she spat out, running forward to beat her small fists against his broad chest. "You made me believe that you could be trusted . . . that you were just as much a prisoner in this place as I am."

"Are you finished?" I asked, disappointed that she hadn't turned all that passion and fury my way. When she stood there—chest heaving from a shortness of breath and her body rigid from indignation—I moved closer to my prisoner. "Knox, take her back to her room and see that she stays there."

"I refuse to leave until I know he's safe." She crossed her arms across her chest, the motion pushing up her breasts. The muscles in her jawline twitched from being tight, her nostrils flaring with insolence. "So help me God, I will rip those chains from him myself if you deny me!"

I didn't know who laughed first—Knox or me. Glancing his way, I saw him shrug, and I chose to instead lean against the wall closest to her. "Then by all means, Mrs. St. James, dazzle us with these feats of strength."

Her face reddened until it rivaled the color of the apples that grew in the estate's orchard.

"What is wrong with you?" she asked, studying me like I was some carnival display she couldn't quite understand. "What could he possibly have done to warrant such treatment?"

She crouched down beside him, her clean hand resting tentatively on his dirty pant leg.

"His business doesn't involve you." It was the only answer she would receive.

Judging by the incredulous look on her face, she wouldn't be accepting it.

"Knox," she pled. It was quaint how she believed he would somehow rally to her side—pitting them both against me. "This man needs sustenance. He may even need a doctor."

"What he needs is none of your concern," he replied, woodenly, without emotion. He glanced my way. "I'll return her to her room and lock the door behind me."

This stirred up wildness in Catriona that was both intoxicating and amusing. It was the kind of expression I imagined she would make in the throes of passion—an expression I wouldn't allow myself to witness. What fascinated me, though, was the belief she still held tightly to. That, somehow, she still had control over her life.

"When you're done, return here so we can deal with this mess." I gestured to the still form with disgust. Our reluctant guest hadn't stirred since I visited his cell late last night, attempting once more to get the information I needed.

"Noooo!" Catriona screeched, kicking out as Knox wrapped his arms around her to carry her out. "You can't treat me this way!"

Her furious tirade continued to echo outside as Knox removed her from the lower levels of the house.

The room descended back into blissful silence.

"Kill me," came the barely audible whisper. "Kill me and be done with it."

I still hadn't managed to uncover exactly who my prisoner was within the gypsy clan I was hunting, but I knew enough to determine he wasn't being truthful.

Sooner or later, with enough incentive, they always confessed.

With enough applied pressure, even the most resilient and determined babbled like babies.

"You wish for death?" I asked, equally quiet. Pacing about the young man, I wondered what it would take to finally break him. Torture had yielded very little result, and frankly, he was beginning to reek from the lack of bathing. "Perhaps I should release you so the wolves can fill their bellies with your flesh."

"It would be an honorable death compared to this." His tone was the same as the long line of others who had sat in that same seat, filled with misplaced pride.

His bitter response filled me with mirth. "You believe yourself honorable?" I barked out an abrupt laugh. "You and your people create monsters, justifying your misuse of magic in the name of family. There is no honor in you or your ancestors." I kicked out at the legs of his chair, gaining his attention.

Black eyes glared up at me—their inky depths revealing how blackened his soul was. There would never be a time when I believed gypsies were a force of greatness in the world. In my mind, the only good gypsy was a dead one.

He tried spitting at me and failed, his mouth too dry to form any kind of spittle. Slumping back in the chair, his head lolled forward, his chin hitting his chest.

"Nikolai," I crooned, walking around him again like he was my prey and I was playing with my dinner. "Your suffering can come to an end . . . you can go home to your family." I trailed my hand across his shoulders, relishing the way he managed to flinch despite being exhausted. "You know what I want. Give me the information, and all this will end. You have my word."

His words came out mumbled, but I still understood them. "The word of the Devil means nothing."

I struck him hard against the side of his head. My patience had limits, and I was growing tired of this song and dance. "Tell me!"

Laughter bubbled out of Nikolai, and with great effort, he lifted his head to stare at me with contempt. "You will never find the cure. You are blood and damnation. Accept it."

I seized hold of his chin, squeezing it tightly between my fingers. Thin lines of blood welled where my fingernails broke his skin, and I resisted the urge to lap up the red liquid. Monster or not, I still had standards, and I refused to feed on gypsy scum.

"You walk a thin line," I threatened, again.

"And you talk too much." He mumbled something in Romani, the sound filled with scorn.

I stopped and got down close to his face—close enough that I could feel his faint breath across my skin.

"You're right." I held his gaze as I made sure he understood my next meaning. "And that is the beauty of your clan. When one won't talk, there are others more fragile who are easier to break. Perhaps a sister . . . mother . . . daughter?"

I studied his reaction, knowing that sooner or later I would hit the mark.

*Daughter.*

He had a daughter.

"I will give your apologies to her. It's unfortunate that you won't get to watch her grow up. That she won't enjoy growing old."

It took a few moments, but the second he understood, he strained against his restraints, heated threats rushing out in a mixture of broken English and Romani.

Reaching forward, I placed both of my hands on the sides of his head and twisted, snapping his neck. He wasn't going to relinquish the information. I wasn't wasting any more time on the dead gypsy.

"Where do you want me to dispose of his body?" Knox had returned in time to see me execute the prisoner.

"With all the snow, you might be hard pressed digging a grave to dump him in." Wiping the grime off my hands, I couldn't help feeling disappointed that once again, we had come up empty-handed. "Ride out a few hours, then drop him into a river or something. Do it far enough away from the estate so as not to raise suspicions."

"And Catriona?"

I let out a heavy sigh. "Inform her that I did as she asked. I gave him his freedom."

It wasn't the complete truth, but it should at least appease her.

I was almost out the door when Knox spoke up.

"Don't give up hope, Marcus. We will find the cure by either finding the gypsies who cursed you or through my experiments. We just need more time."

Nodding, I left him to take care of the body, trudging back up the stairs to my office.

Alone.

# CHAPTER 7

*L*ife was about ritual—at least that's what mine had been reduced to. The carefree days of my youth were but a distant memory now, and it was often painful dwelling on what might have been.

Making my way to Knox's study was part of the nightly routine that dictated everything—superseding temptation and any form of nostalgia. Just once, I wished I could abandon all the safeguards I'd placed in my life, and simply *be*.

Free to be whoever the hell I chose to be and not the persona—the monster—I had become.

Ever since Catriona had moved into the house, these kinds of thoughts plagued me, causing waves of self-doubt to surface from the emotions I kept buried deep inside me.

It didn't pay to feel or have a heart anymore. Every decision I made was one of life or death. When it came to seeking vengeance—pure unadulterated revenge—feelings simply got in the way. I'd learned quickly once I started changing into the blood drinker those two women cursed me to become, that I would drown trying to hold tight to my humanity.

It was one of the first things I relinquished of my old life—like a snake shedding its skin. What was needed was the ability to be one hundred percent ruthless, to be such a force of nature that even the trees would bend to my will.

I lived in a world now saturated in deviousness and darkness. It was one where you were either the predator or the prey—the invincible or the destructible.

What was left of that former Marcus wasn't enough to brave falling in love. There was barely enough of my true self to maintain the friendship I had with Knox. He knew that and accepted it anyway.

What begun by chance had evolved into a symbiotic relationship where we both benefited. I'd found him a homeless beggar on the streets of London, and there was something about the young Phineas Knox that whispered his value. I'd learned not to judge others too quickly, and it had definitely paid off.

Down on his luck, his tall form lanky and thin from malnutrition, Knox hadn't thought twice about my offer to become his employer. All he saw was a way out of the cutthroat streets—a way to always have food in his stomach and a warm place to sleep.

I saw an urchin who was street smart—someone who could slip by unnoticed—a boy who would know the value of loyalty.

So it came as a complete surprise when he confided that he'd been an apprentice to an obscure alchemist. That brand of magic and science was a mystery to me, but something had impressed on me that, one day, such knowledge would prove useful.

It didn't matter that he claimed he'd burnt his master's home down from a spell gone awry. I overlooked the way the tips of his ears reddened as he confessed his complete lack of skill—his mouth full of the fresh warm bread I'd given him.

Knox had looked me dead in the eye—every inch the man he was beneath the grime—and vowed that should I give him a chance, he would never fail me. He would always serve me to the best of his abilities.

Here we were, after all this time, and he'd honored his word.

There were a few small incidents where he'd set fire to the bed in the connecting room, and then to the draperies hanging heavily over the only two windows in his study. Those things were inconsequential compared to the work he slaved over at the desk.

Knox had preserved my sanity, and for that, he would always have a home with me—servant or not.

Knocking briefly on the door, I didn't wait for him to welcome me into his sanctuary. It was a given that no door would ever be barred against me. There would never be any secrets. He knew mine, and I knew his—what little there was to know.

"I wondered where you were," came a deep baritone voice. "I would've brought the elixir to you, Marcus, but as you can see . . ." Knox waved his hand over the large wooden bench he'd made to work on. The surface was covered with all manner of tools he needed—glassware, candles, endless stacks of papers with weird symbols and scratching on them, empty ink bottles, and herbs.

I crinkled my nose. How he managed to work in such chaos was beyond me, but he'd once said that all creative geniuses preferred working in a mess. It quieted the voices in his head, apparently. I didn't argue.

"Please tell me that stench isn't for me."

While I was his master, I recognized this was his domain. Careful not to disturb anything, my gaze skimmed over the work in front of him. Knox didn't bother covering it up—he knew full well I couldn't read the alchemist symbols.

He let out a chuckle. Pushing back from the bench, the wooden stool scraping across the bare floor, Knox picked up a glass filled with thick, red liquid. That was another thing we removed from his study—carpet. We considered it a wise choice considering the amount of liquids and potions he spilled on an almost daily basis.

"Would you prefer the alternative?" he fired back, holding out the drink.

This was how I drank my blood. It was mostly human with different concoctions added—whatever Knox was testing to see if it would help curb my cravings and keep the beast at bay.

Before his help, I'd resorted to slipping into town every night and gorging until I couldn't swallow another mouthful of blood. My hunger all but consumed me, and there were still whisperings in the nearby counties of a monster that scoured the countryside in search of new victims.

I'd left death and carnage in my wake. There were times when I'd been too lazy to cover up my kills, launching the town or village into mass hysteria. Banners were placed all around with generous rewards for anyone who could bring the killer to justice.

Once I knew that Knox could be trusted, I'd confessed who I truly was, and he'd set about trying to find a cure for the curse. He'd been adamant that perhaps alchemy could hold the answers, and that I couldn't wait to find the gypsies.

And here we were. I was drinking his god-awful elixirs, and my appetite for blood was under control. Unfortunately, he still hadn't figured out a way to fully restore me.

He was the only thing in which I had any faith left. Sooner or later, he would be successful. He was too stubborn to admit defeat.

"Sometimes I miss the pleasure of sinking my teeth into something warm," I murmured, bracing myself to take my first swallow. "The way the blood flowed freely into my mouth . . . the ecstatic way it left a blazing trail of fire down my throat." I took a deep breath and decided to swallow the contents in one gulp.

The sensation was a meager substitute to the real thing, but it did its job. The uneasiness I always felt began to subside as it heated my stomach, and the loud, growly presence in my head grew quiet.

"Was this new?" I asked, placing the now empty glass beside Knox on the bench. "There was something . . . different about it." I gestured to the red liquid still staining the cup.

He nodded. "Gold. I added gold flakes to it with the hopes that as it builds up in your system, I may be able to alter your organs. By perfecting *you*, I will have created a vessel that can transform to whatever I wish it to be."

Like always, whenever he tried explaining the science behind his experimenting, my head began to throb. "So, I'm essentially a creature you're testing your theories on." It was more of a fact than a question.

Knox paused long enough from swirling about some clear liquid in his bowl to glance at me. "You disagree?"

It had been a long time since I'd lingered after taking my nightly tonic. He was more used to me gruffly accepting the blood, drinking it, and then leaving in a similar manner.

Yet here I was—trying to start a conversation and interrupting him from working.

"I trust you, Phineas," I assured him. "I sometimes wish I understood exactly what it is you do down here." Picking up one of the loose leaves of paper, I turned it about to show him. "This looks like utter nonsense, but if you tell me this brings us closer to removing this damn curse, that'll be enough for me. It will have to be enough."

Abandoning his work for a moment, Knox turned about, his hands resting on his knees. "I gave you my word that I wouldn't stop until I helped free you. You saved me that night in London, and I owe you a life debt." He chuckled as he took the paper back. "As for these, even the failures are a step forward. I don't possess the same skill and clarity of my former master, but what I lack in expertise, I make up for in sheer stubbornness."

"And gold flakes are the latest?" It felt weird knowing the precious metal was now pumping through my veins.

He shrugged. "It's just a thought. In alchemy, gold is considered a source that promotes human renewal and regeneration. My theory is that by infusing your very organs and blood with it, perhaps it will trigger that transformation within you—that it will help your spirit fight against the evilness of the curse, and triumph." Knox glanced at the empty glass, his brows furrowed in thought. "Again, that's the notion I'm exploring right now."

"And here I thought you were merely throwing in different ingredients to see which one made me sick," I teased, suddenly struck with appreciation for my friend. He had grown to be much more than someone who served me. I gave his study one more sweeping look. "Do you require anything?"

It wasn't uncommon for Knox to come to me with a long list of the items he required. I learned not to question some of them, especially if they would end up in my elixirs.

I could already see his focus returning to his work.

"Yes. I may need to go to London for the supplies." He wasn't even looking at me now. Whatever he'd been writing had snared his attention again, and his silence was a loud indication that our discussion was over.

"I may join you then." There was a certain seer I'd been trying to gain an audience with, but each time, I'd been denied. Knox wasn't the only one who refused to admit defeat. I was determined to finally meet with the infamous Lady Hannah.

Knox mumbled something in return.

One more nightly ritual was complete.

As I headed toward the door, he called out again, surprising me. "One of the added ingredients in your drink will help you dream walk. Just in case you wanted to visit anyone . . . understand anyone."

His comment stopped me dead in my tracks.

Dream walk?

"You don't need me to explain that, Marcus. You now have the ability to visit someone while they're asleep."

"Why?" I asked, curious how he'd deduced that. I didn't sleep very often, and therefore, didn't dream. I wasn't interested in making social calls that way either.

It was his turn to look at me, bewildered. "I had the thought the other night when I went to dispose of the gypsy. What if instead of trying to break his body and spirit, we attack from a place where he wouldn't be expecting it? A man can tolerate unimaginable pain if he believes it's for a just cause. In our dreams, we are more vulnerable . . . more susceptible to coercion."

I was impressed. Knox's reasoning was sound, and if it worked, could save a lot of time. In fact, it was a brilliant idea that I hoped prove fruitful. "I can't wait to see the results then. We'll bring home a subject to test it on."

The corners of his mouth curled in a mischievous way, and I

instantly saw he had an ulterior motive. "Why wait? There's someone who resides under this roof you could understand better." And with that, Knox looked up in the direction of Catriona's bedchambers.

"No," I retorted, my response loud and forceful. "Absolutely not."

"Do you have so many friends, Marcus, that you can't stomach to nurture another ally?" I had his full attention again, which made me wonder how long he'd been preparing to tell me this. "I am good at what I do, but there are certain places even I can't enter. Don't you think it a good idea to have Catriona help you break this curse as well? Women talk—a lot. They gossip. Why not befriend her and see what she can uncover?"

I loathed the suggestion with a fiery passion. The thought of confessing my secrets to the female forced into my keeping felt intolerable. It would require my being vulnerable with her—discarding the persona I'd adopted with her and being someone . . . softer.

"She thinks me a monster."

"She only sees what *you* show her. You already know my thoughts on that." Knox gave me a shrewd stare. "She should never have been placed in the role of an enemy."

"Who is the master here?" I thundered, uncomfortable with the way the conversation was going. It wasn't because I thought it was ridiculous. No, slowly but surely, I was beginning to see the sense in it.

"You, but that doesn't change the fact that my advice bears consideration."

I didn't speak another word. His words bounced around in my head, and no amount of refusal and denial on my part dimmed the truth.

She would make a better ally than enemy.

If she was going to remain here with me, it would be better that I find a use for her, instead of letting all that pent-up frustration and hostility percolate. Sooner or later, it would need an outlet, and I had a sinking suspicion Catriona would level me with her anger.

Part of me wanted to witness that.

But common sense won.

"Let me consider it," I muttered, heading for the door again.

"All you need do is think of her before sleeping and you'll find yourself where she is."

I'd sworn I wouldn't rest until I was fully human again and my cursers dead by my hand. If dream walking helped me accomplish that —if it finally uncovered the answers I'd spent over a decade looking for —then it was time to win over my wife.

# CHAPTER 8

*S*leeping was such a foreign concept to me, something that I required less of as the years passed. Mostly, I reserved it for those moments where I needed a break from the drudgery of everyday living. The brief respite seemed to soothe my nerves around the edges, making it possible not to completely lose my mind.

Now I was seeking sleep for a different reason, and I wasn't quite sure how I felt about that. Once upon a time, I thought knowing the innermost thoughts and feelings of others would be a useful trick to have, but I still wasn't convinced understanding Catriona was a good idea.

There was so much that could go wrong. Tampering with another person's psyche, especially when they were vulnerable, could only complicate matters further. Something told me that my wife wouldn't appreciate the violation, either.

But my curiosity, once stoked, was a hard thing to quell.

Laying back on my bed, I tried to make myself as comfortable as possible. Slowly I could feel my muscles releasing their tension, and the first telltale signs of sleep started trickling through my body.

It wouldn't be long now before I ventured into unknown territory.

"Think of her," I whispered beneath my breath. Images of the beautiful brunette surfaced, and despite the countless times she'd irritated me, there was no denying that my wife was in fact an extremely attractive woman.

I pictured the way her dark locks seemed to have a mind of their own—hanging in long curls that framed her pretty face. I hated admitting that my fingers often itched to tangle in the thickness, missing the way it had felt that day back in my office when we first met. What had started as a way to undermine her confidence had turned around and bitten me hard, because it was often all I could think about.

I wanted to trace the soft curve of her face, relishing the way heat flooded her cheeks at my touch. She was unspoiled and virtuous—the brief taste I'd stolen confirming she would open up like a beautiful flower, each petal begging to be admired.

Her red lips held my attention regardless of what she was saying. Whether it was the way she softly sang to herself when she thought no one was watching or the way they pursed when she disapproved of something I had done, they drew me to her. Her mouth—her kiss— would be as intoxicating as a flagon of ale. I doubted there was a man alive who would escape becoming drunk on such a taste.

But it was her temperament that drew me in like a moth to a flame. She was both fire and tenderness—chaos and stability— strength and fragility. She was a walking contradiction to me, because one moment she would flay me on the spot with her shrewd brown eyes, and in the next breath, gently cradle a wounded bird in her hands. The way she viewed the world was at complete odds with how I had been forced to see it.

She saw injustice and sought to correct it by showing kindness to others.

I saw injustice and wanted to rain down blood and violence until I gained my revenge.

Drowsiness beckoned until I couldn't keep my eyes open. With one last murmur of her name, the world dissolved, and I found myself someplace strange.

"Marcus?" The breathlessness of her voice caused a ripple of awareness to pulse through me. She'd never spoken to me like that before, and the part I had tried denying flared back into existence. I felt greedy for such softness.

"Catriona," I replied, finding her sitting on a brick wall covered with green moss and vines. "Where are we?"

I couldn't tell if this was a figment of her imagination or if she was visiting a place she knew.

"The ruins where Lancelot and Guinevere would meet secretly." There was a wistfulness about her as she looked around with fondness that told me she was a romantic at heart. "At least, that's what I've told myself. I'm sure this is merely the long-forgotten home of someone." Catriona stroked the brick wall she was still perched on. "But I like to come here and think."

She gave me a pointed glance that told me I was often the subject of such musings.

I slowly started walking around, noting how secluded it was, half believing that this was actually a place that lovers rendezvoused— stealing kisses and heated embraces away from the prying eyes of the world.

"I could see that," I confessed, gingerly touching a rich green vine with budding white flowers dotting it. "We live in a world where the forbidden intrigues us."

"And where we can't always act on our passions."

Her response caused me to stop long enough to study her next. "You have passions, Catriona?"

Females in society didn't have the luxury of acting upon their own, let alone acknowledging openly that they were stirred by the same instincts and cravings men were.

"Why are you here, Marcus?" she gently pressed. "I've never dreamed of you before, yet here you are as though you belong here with me."

Like a queen on a throne, she hadn't moved since I'd come across her, the height of the broken wall making it so she sat higher than me.

With the light shining from behind, she looked ethereal.

"How do you know you haven't brought me here yourself?" I

countered, unable to keep myself from being somewhat honest with her. I held her gaze as long as I could before lowering my eyes.

I was completely out of my element here and unsure of how to proceed. In the waking world, I would exert my dominance and force her to cower and answer whatever questions I had. I wasn't used to being asked my intentions.

"So, at last, you are my prisoner." Her smile was genuine and void of any malice. I couldn't say I would be as gracious if the roles had been reversed. "Seeing as you are intruding on my dream, I would say I also hold all the control." A twinkle sparked in her eyes, revealing a side of mischievousness I hadn't seen before either.

"So it seems," I replied and bent at the waist, offering my respect. "What would you wish of me, my lady?"

I added a flourish with my hand and was rewarded with the soft tinkling of her laughter. Another sound I hadn't known I needed until this precise moment.

I had nothing to lose by dropping the persona I held in the waking world. If there was ever an opportunity to lower my guard and simply enjoy something carefree and innocent, it was now.

Sadness skated across her features. "No matter how much I would love for this to be real . . . for us to hold a genuine conversation where we mutually liked one another . . ."

A stray tear fell from her lashes. It killed me not to reach over and capture it with my thumb. These emotions—the foreignness of feeling compassion after all these many years—churned up confusion inside me. Bit by bit, I could feel the façade I had cloaked myself with fall, until all that was left was . . . me.

I didn't like it.

I hated it.

But I also embraced it, stood in awe of it—of knowing such affection was still possible for a monster like me.

"Pretend with me then," I encouraged, and finally moved from where I'd been standing to her. Knowing this was only a dream, I bravely took her hand and held it between my own. The warmth of her skin felt real enough to send a shiver up my spine.

Warning bells sounded in my head—cautioning that to proceed would only result in heartache and would be dangerously reckless. In truth, the last time I had allowed myself to feel anything remotely close to the romantic feelings swirling about in my chest, I'd woken to find myself holding a dead body in my arms, and the wrath of a gypsy clan dragged down upon me.

*Drop her hand*, a voice screamed inside me. *Wake up. The way before you is folly and you know it.*

My fingers twitched as if they longed to obey, but I held on tighter. This was what I had been secretly craving—yearning for. Human connection. Revenge had kept me warm throughout the years, but it hadn't brought me a speck of solace.

I was bone weary of constantly fighting.

Just once, I wanted to see what it felt like to find that peace in another.

"Catriona," I murmured, finally cupping the side of her face, my thumb softly circling over her skin. "We are quite impossible."

She nodded, holding herself still as though with one wrong move, this would all fade away. I could see the questions bubbling up in her eyes, each one waiting to be asked. I was sure she was biting her tongue, unsure about whether to give them voice, or whether she should remain silent—waiting to see where this moment might lead us.

"I never wished this life for you. In another lifetime, I know I could grow to love you deeply, to delight in growing old with you. You are quite a remarkable woman . . ." I struggled to find the right words, my tongue tripping over my own thoughts. "A treasure to any man."

"Then why do you act so abominably toward me? Why must we be enemies?" The earnestness in her voice was almost strong enough to break me. There was nothing more I wanted in this moment than to promise her things would change and that the happiness she desperately longed for could be ours.

But we weren't part of some fairy tale of star-crossed lovers, fighting against the odds to be with each other. My reality was set in stone—at least until Knox and I found a cure. By then, it might be too late for anything to grow between Catriona and me.

"What do you want from me?" I finally asked, holding the side of her cheek as I tilted her head to look deep into her eyes. "Ask now, because once this dream is over, what we want can never be."

Catriona slowly slipped from the wall and stood before me, her hands hanging by her side, fingers loosely gripping her nightgown's material. She looked so unbelievably small amongst her surroundings, but her request revealed the magnitude of her heart.

"Love me, Marcus. Even if it's just for the briefest of seconds. Let me have something to hold on to once this is over." Tears began to fall again. "I know I mean nothing to you, but please."

For some reason, her request came as a shock. I'd expected her to beg for her freedom or to have more control in the waking world—to even be friends. That made more sense to me than a request for love, no matter how temporary and fleeting it was.

I responded instinctively, pulling her into my arms as I rested my forehead on hers. It was the most intimate position I'd ever been in, regardless of how many times I'd shared my bed with another. It was as though our spirits gently spoke—communicating the emotions I knew I couldn't even dare to voice.

"You don't know what you ask."

"Am I so unlovable that you can't even muster the smallest of sympathy for me? I am lonely, Marcus. I am your wife in word only . . . and even that is viewed scornfully by you. Give me something that I can hold on to when we return and you . . ."

Again, she struggled to complete her fevered petition. Her body relaxed into mine as a signal that she was done trying to convince me. She was accepting that any hope for a relationship was a feeble one. I'd watched that belief disappear in reality, and now . . . now I was witnessing its death in her dreams.

It was that realization that obliterated any kind of resistance in me. Let them believe I was a monster, because I knew I played my role masterfully, and their hateful opinions meant nothing to me.

But hers . . . somehow, along the way, she had come to matter.

"Catriona," I whispered again, the thudding of my heart loud in my ears. "Will just one moment be enough? I can't give you what you want, but if a small token will appease you, then . . ."

My words faded away as I cradled her face in both hands.

What I was about to do was extremely dangerous. Not for her, but for me. It threatened to unravel any hope of being the particular beast needed to exact my revenge.

Love and hate couldn't exist within a person at the same time.

Catriona claimed that it would be enough for her—that she would cherish whatever morsel I offered, but the truth was this:

I didn't know if it would be enough for me.

Could one more taste last a lifetime?

Lowering my head, my mouth hovered over hers, lips barely touching. We were both lonely. We both craved an intimacy that had so far been withheld from us. It made sense to find that comfort with each other.

But at what cost?

Was loving Catriona worth abandoning my thirst for retribution?

Which battle could I live with—the violence and singular focus required to hunt my cursers to the ends of the earth, or the agonizing restraint needed to ignore my need for this remarkable woman?

She had shown no fear when facing me, a man who had no qualms about treating her worse than the horses in his stables. She'd shown incredible courage, facing days filled with the unknown, her life no longer her own to control.

Knox had been right. I'd been wrong this whole time. Perhaps trusting Catriona and giving in to the feelings we both shared could only bring happiness to my dark existence.

Maybe.

Hopefully.

I couldn't think any more. Closing the distance between us, I seized her mouth and surrendered. I kissed her as though everything depended on the electricity passing between us. I poured every piece of me into it, and she replied with her own intensity.

I was drowning in her.

I lost myself in her.

For the briefest of seconds, I would've given up everything for her —my mission, the search for a cure, every twisted thought that had consumed me and shaped me into the man who now clung to her like a lifeline.

It wasn't until a thought brazenly infiltrated my mind that I dared to pull away, breaking the seal of our mouths.

We both stood there with heaving chests, desperately trying to slow our breathing, lips bruised from our outburst of passion. Her hair was mussed, and I longed to drag her back against me, to embrace her and never let go.

But there was no denying that one traitorous thought.

*She doesn't know who you truly are.*

And with that singular sentence, I woke up with a start.

# CHAPTER 9

*I* couldn't remember the last time I'd come into this room.

Catriona lay peacefully under the covers, still locked in the dream we'd shared. The dwindling flame of a candle slowly burned, offering a small amount of light in the darkened bedchamber.

*Turn around and leave*, an inner voice cried, trying to reason with my heart. *This path will only lead to misery.*

I agreed with the thought blaring inside my head, but it didn't prevent me from completely entering her sanctuary and closing the door behind me. The effects of the kiss we'd exchanged—her plea for something more than merely coexisting in the same house—all these things wreaked havoc over my senses.

It felt as though my entire being was at war with itself, and for the first time, I was undecided how to move forward. It didn't matter that I'd instantly rushed to her side, hoping to continue the kiss that had ravaged my self-control. The truth still rang loud and clear.

Catriona St. James had no idea with whom she was begging to have a meaningful relationship. Whatever ideals she imagined while she hid away in this room—whatever fantasies she concocted in her lover's dream hideaway—I could never be that man for her.

The sooner she understood why it was impossible, the faster she could relinquish those expectations and accept the bitter hand Fate had dealt us both.

I needed to wake her and take her to the only place I knew that would remove any confusion and release me from the temptation of wanting what we couldn't have.

She let out a faint sigh and shifted slowly, not resting until she found a comfortable spot. It felt like a sin to wake her—to shatter the tranquility that graced her beautiful features and replace it with one of revulsion and disgust.

There would be no gazing up at me, no sinking into my embrace, once she'd heard my complete confession. She would be confined to a doomed marriage and left to live out the rest of her days in bleakness, always hoping for the one thing she couldn't obtain.

"Catriona," I whispered, nudging her arm to rouse her. I was on the verge of losing my nerve, of bargaining with my conscience that a few more minutes of ignorant bliss would be worth it.

A coward's choice, but it was all I could do not to take a seat and continue watching her sleep. Such beauty right before me was a heady invitation to refuse.

I repeated her name again, this time louder.

Thick eyelashes fluttered open, and it took her a few moments to completely wake up. I knew the instant she recognized she wasn't alone, because she quickly sat up and tugged the bedding up under her chin, as though it would protect her from my cruelty.

She was no longer the Catriona from the dream.

I mourned that it was seeing me that destroyed it.

"Mr. St. James?" she asked, her voice shaky. Strands of her thick black hair were messed from her pillow, and I watched in fascination, wanting to smooth it out for her.

"There is something I want to show you," I answered, shaking myself to dislodge the lovesick thoughts that threatened to addle my brain. This was the very reason why I didn't want to get close to her— to allow myself to feel anything toward Catriona beside obligation. "Come, you'll need to put on your shoes and an overcoat."

She didn't move. She simply stared at me as though I was some apparition delivering a message that made little sense.

"Did you hear me?" I asked, this time going to retrieve her coat myself. "There is a conversation we must have that is long overdue. All I ask is that you hear me out and make your decision once you've heard all the details." Holding out the jacket, I waited as she quietly slipped on her shoes.

It wasn't until she'd finished buttoning up her winter coat that she spoke. "Can this not wait until the morning?" Her words were muffled behind her hand as she stifled a yawn. As she came closer to me, she sniffed the air. "Are you drunk? Is that why you're dragging me from my bed?" She had the sense to look apprehensive.

I did my best to feed her fears. "You need to be afraid, Catriona." It was difficult not to take offense when she flinched away from my extended hand. "I won't hurt you. You have my word."

With a trust I wasn't worthy of, she placed her hands firmly in mine, and nodded. "Then show me, Marcus."

We walked through the house in absolute silence, neither of us breathing a word. Only our footsteps echoed in the still hallway as I slowly led her out through the kitchen door into the cool early-morning air. The sun had yet to peep above the tree line, and the chirping birds that often sang their song each morning were still nestled in their nests.

There was a crispness that left me feeling alive. It was chilly enough to set goose bumps across my skin.

"Slow down, Marcus," she begged, tripping over the hem of her nightgown and clutching my arm for balance. "I'm not familiar with the path we're on, and I don't want to fall."

In my haste, I'd forgotten that she often kept to the house and inner gardens. I'd chosen the place where I went to reflect specifically for that reason. Not even Knox ventured this way.

"Only a little farther, and then I'll explain everything," I promised, and gripped her hand tighter. The hero in a story might have gathered her up in his arms, offering to carry her safely, but I was already skating on thin ice. Even if Catriona was able to look past the curse, I wasn't her hero.

It was everything I could do not to be her own personal villain.

There was always a solemn hush whenever I entered the clearing, and it was no different now. It was only a small glen, but surrounded by tall trees, and with the full moon shining above, I was reminded why I chose to build the gravesite for Primrose here.

Her body was buried far from here, but I'd erected the gravestone as a reminder of what had been lost that night. I came here every day to offer my penance for somehow playing a part in her death. I'd eventually remembered being knocked across the head by cutthroats, after trying to protect Primrose from their advances. It truly had been a case of being in the wrong place at the wrong time, but I'd still been there.

I'd spent hours trying to convince myself that I'd done everything I could to defend her honor. The strangers had spewed out such filth at the young gypsy woman, I was surprised God didn't strike them down for such depravity.

Many prayers had been offered up as I knelt beside the simple stone carving, pouring my heart out with the hopes that somehow God would show mercy and pity my feeble attempts.

In the beginning, I came looking for redemption.

All I had left was bitter prayers that I would one day meet my maker having found my vengeance.

"Who is she?"

It was my turn to jump. I'd forgotten she was standing there, my thoughts consuming me again.

My voiced cracked from thick emotion. "Her name was Primrose."

Catriona stepped between me and the headstone, trailing her fingers lightly across the top. "Did you love her? Is that why you can't love me?"

She squinted at me, hoping to catch the truth through my reaction to her questions.

It was on the tip of my tongue to lie to her, to sugarcoat what I wanted to tell her, so I would at least be seen in a favorable light. But that wasn't the reason behind me bringing her here.

Just as the night gave way to the day—the moon setting as the sun rose—I couldn't remain in the shadows with her anymore. I needed her to see me . . . to see all the horrible flaws and choices I'd made. Nothing was as brutal as that first ray of light, because there was no hiding from its blinding honesty.

Guiding her to the wooden bench I'd spent many evenings sitting on, I paced back and forth in front of her, suddenly nervous.

"Listen to what I have to say in its entirety. Once I'm done, I will answer whatever questions you might have. I only ask that you reserve judgment until the last detail has been confessed."

She nodded in agreement. "What's brought about this change in heart, Marcus?" There was a soft smile when she realized she'd already disobeyed my request. "I only ask so I don't dwell on it."

"How were your dreams tonight?" I countered, bracing myself for her anger. "Did you enjoy your time in the ruins?"

Her mouth dropped open with astonishment, and she shrank back against the bench, her hands clutching at her gown. Each time she began to speak, Catriona shook her head, dismissing the thought.

"I took a potion so I could visit you in your dreams," I continued, studying her to see how she might react. She appeared eerily calm and not the feisty woman who'd threatened to sneak into my room at night and chain me to my bed so she could escape. "Catriona?" Her silence was unnerving.

"That was real?" she finally asked, her eyes wide as saucers. "That means we . . ." Her fingers pressed against her lips as if she was remembering the passion between us.

I nodded. "Invading your dreams is one of many sins I need to confess to you." I took a step toward her and thought better of it. I didn't trust myself right now, and as my hunger flared deep in my gut, I realized I should've gone to Knox for fortification before attempting this heavy conversation. "Will you listen to what I need to say?"

It looked like she didn't trust herself to respond, either. Nodding, she folded her hands in her lap and gave me her full attention.

Suddenly at a loss for words, I glanced over to Primrose's memorial, praying that somewhere in her afterlife, she could see I was trying to do the right thing.

Taking in a deep breath, and with the morning's first rays brightening the sky, I then prayed for courage to see this retelling through to the devastating end.

For Catriona.

For Primrose.

For the broken pieces of my soul.

WAITING for her to speak was an exercise in agony.

I had divulged it all, leaving no detail untold as I gave a faithful account of that night in the alleyway, of Primrose's death and the subsequent cursing by her kin.

I described the person I had transformed myself into—the reasoning behind embracing my new life as a blood drinker—how easy it had been to become cruel and hostile to those around me.

I spoke about that night, how in desperation and anguish I'd vowed my most solemn oath of vengeance. I shared each failed attempt in finding the gypsy clan. I spoke of the carnage I had wielded —the bodies and blood I had consumed in my pursuits.

I had resembled a feral animal in those days before Knox planted those few seeds of faith that he could find the answers I needed. Story after story, I confessed my thirst and hunger for blood and gore, of leaving trails of dead behind me, of being the very killer many in the country whispered about.

I didn't stop—even when her gasps grew louder and louder—or the look of horror remained across her face. With each syllable, the possibility of ever kissing her again, of truly being a husband to her, faded away until it blinked out of existence.

This was what I wanted.

I wanted her to see me for the beast I was, and to give up her futile attempts to tame me.

I wanted her to run away from me screaming.

I wanted her to declare her own oath—that for as long as she drew breath, she would fight to stop me harming innocent people.

There was so much I needed from her—from her reaction—but it didn't keep the whole ordeal from feeling like I was slowly being gutted, one agonizing cut at a time.

I needed her to loathe my very presence.

I needed her to curse my birth and wish for my speedy death.

Yet she did neither, and that was what devastated me.

She didn't offer her condemnation nor her acceptance.

I wasn't foolish enough to think she'd give me her forgiveness, but something—anything but her silence—would've been enough.

Finally, she let out a faint breath, and looked at me. "Why tell me all this?"

Her stare unmanned me. "Because it's the only thing I can give you, Catriona. You showed me your heart in your dreams, and I felt you deserved the same in return. While I can never give anyone my love and affection, I can at least help you understand why."

She slowly nodded as if she was struggling to digest it all. "Well, I appreciate that, Marcus."

Her brow crinkled from the heavy thoughts mulling about inside her head. At least, I assumed they were heavy. I knew mine were.

"Do you have any questions for me?" I asked, hoping that might alleviate some of the tension. "I promised you I would answer them all as truthfully as I can."

"You drink blood." Fact.

I bobbed my head.

She nervously raised her hand to her throat. "Do you want to drink mine?"

I took a step back to grant her some space. "There was a time when I would've taken from you, whenever I wanted." Her eyes widened again, and I almost expected her to get up and flee. "However, Knox has made it so I only need to feed once a day. He procures the blood I need and then adds his special ingredients to it. It enables me to control that part of me without becoming a ravaging beast."

That surprised her. "You want to live like this?" Her incredulous tone was understandable.

"All I had was my honor when I walked into that alley with Primrose. I wasn't guilty of the crimes they accused me of, yet they cursed me anyway. They reduced me to this." I didn't hide the bitterness I felt, smacking my hands against my chest in anger. "Justice demands to be appeased. They will pay for what they've stolen from me."

I wanted to smooth out the permanent wrinkle on her brow. "In one breath you speak of honor and justice, yet you thirst for your revenge. They are at odds with each other—you can't have revenge *and* remain honorable."

"Watch me," I fired back, my own annoyance flaring. "Endure what I have and see whether you still believe that. I didn't ask for this life, but I will use whatever *gifts* it has given me to claim some semblance of peace."

She had the audacity to laugh. "You call this peace, Marcus? Let go of your need to make those who've harmed you pay. Embrace this new life and make the best of it. Imagine the great things you could do with your extended life. Think of the legacy you could leave in your wake . . . of being someone who rises above the harshness of life and makes the world a better place."

I shook my head, already dismissing her words as folly. "Can you not see that this is the path I am destined to walk? I used to believe I held some control over what Fate did . . . that I chose the life I wanted. If there was one thing the curse has taught me, it's that I was a fool, and in order to survive, I needed to kill that side of me."

"Then I pity you, Marcus, I truly do. You're wasting the chance given you to find meaning and purpose."

Anger continued to bubble up inside me. While I'd granted her the freedom to talk to me as she wanted, to ask her questions, it still rankled. Her fear I could handle. Her disappointment and disgust were expected.

It was her pity that irritated me, because I didn't need her sorrow.

"This is why we can never have the kind of relationship you yearn for."

"So, you chose to act like a barbarian because you felt I was too weak and feeble-minded to understand your plight?" She finally stood and approached me, placing her hand over my chest. "Do you really think so little of me?"

It was my turn to be speechless.

"Thank you for confiding in me. Your secret is safe with me." Patting my chest affectionately, she left me with a smile that tugged at my heartstrings again. "Let us be friends." And with that, she kissed my cheek and turned to head back to the house.

Right before she disappeared from my sight, I found my voice.

"Catriona, thank you," I called out. Then, as a new thought arose, I threw caution to the wind. "Prepare to journey to London later this morning."

She stilled ever so slightly, then nodded.

Falling onto the bench, exhausted, I couldn't help but wonder if this had been yet another mistake in a long line of many.

Friends.

It was more than I deserved.

Much more.

# CHAPTER 10

*M*rs. Pickering was worth every pound her services demanded.

Upon our arrival in London, I quickly sent Knox to see whether the popular seamstress would see us. Those who recommended her were adamant there was little chance of her granting our request because of how highly in demand she was. I'd listened to them all attentively, but I also recognized a greater truth.

Lengthy waiting lists could often be obliterated when enough money was placed on the table. I had extremely deep pockets and no problem spending the wealth I had accumulated.

Sitting on the gold brocaded chaise longue in the corner of her workshop, I couldn't keep the smug expression from settling across my face.

Catriona had been so anxious about being dressed by the woman who boasted about a client list containing some of the most elite aristocrats in our country. Hell, Mrs. Pickering had even adorned the king and his queen with her fineries.

After glaring at my speechless companion, I reminded her that her new wardrobe was a gift from me—my way of showing her how truly sorry I was for my former treatment of her.

As far as I was concerned, the moment we were able to, I would order a bonfire to destroy the tacky clothes I'd forced on her.

"What do you think, Mr. St. James? Does your wife not look stunning in this emerald green dress?" The older woman stood back from her creation, gesturing to Catriona, who was raised up on a wide stool so Mrs. Pickering and her apprentice, Harriet, could move about easily. "With the rich darkness of her hair, and her flawless skin, you may wish to hire a guard to keep this one safe." Gazing up at Catriona, the seamstress continued. "You, my darling, are quite stunning."

She rattled off a long string of instructions to her apprentice, who in turn faithfully jotted it all down on a small pad. I'd told her the outfits I believed Catriona would need and that she was to spare no expense.

She'd simply chuckled softly and patted me on the arm like I was a child. "My dear, I have no doubt that you are quite accomplished at what you do. However, you don't see me come into your office and tell you how to do your work. Do you doubt my abilities? My skills?" She cocked an eyebrow as if daring me to challenge her. "I didn't think so. You've come to me because you heard I am the best. Perhaps you should've left with your manservant?"

Answers bounced around in my mind, but something warned me that this was not a woman to argue with. Resigning myself to the corner, I'd spent most of the past few hours watching the process.

And watching my wife . . . who wasn't truly my wife . . . who was barely a newly formed friend . . . the woman who continued to complicate my life.

"What do you think?" Catriona asked, chewing her bottom lip as she twisted, the dress swishing about her. "You don't think it's too elaborate for spending each day at the estate?"

I heard the question within the question she asked.

Why was I going to such an extreme when all she would ever see were the walls within my home? So far, I had not taken her out into society, refusing any invitations to balls and dinner parties that were extended.

People would always be curious about me—the reclusive heir of

Smithersby Field—but she was something else entirely. Rumors had labeled me a confirmed bachelor after my constant refusal to court the local beauties. Yet, here I was, married.

They wanted to meet *her* with the hopes of understanding how she'd managed to tie herself to such an affluent family.

*Let them wonder*, I silently grumbled.

I nodded my agreement. "You look beautiful, Catriona."

I added a smile to my words, hoping that it didn't reveal the true depths of my feelings. She wasn't just beautiful—she was extraordinary.

She flinched as Harriet accidently pricked her with a long dressmaking pin. It earned the poor young girl a slap from Mrs. Pickering, and the admonishment that should she spoil the fabric with blood, it would come out of her meager wage.

The mention of blood tugged at my senses, and my mouth watered. The elixir Knox had brought the previous night had all but left my system, and oddly, my hunger had roared back with a vengeance. There might not be time enough to wait until we returned home.

There was a knock at the door, and to my relief, Knox entered, his eyes glued to Catriona's svelte figure on display.

Whistling softly, he dragged his gaze away from her, and approached me. "Marcus, we have a problem." He crouched down beside me so he could whisper. "I tried to get you an audience with her, but she is unmovable. I couldn't even gain entrance to her home to ask her personally and share your plight with her."

It was as I thought. We had been lucky with Mrs. Pickering, but meeting with the infamous seer of London proved to be impossible. People came from near and far to have Lady Hannah read their futures. I already knew mine, but I had desperately hoped she could grant us some insight into the curse I bore.

"Perhaps I should try," I answered, already moving to stand. As pleasant as the view had been, Catriona's new wardrobe would not restore me to the man I was. It wouldn't help me gain my revenge. It was simply a means of distraction.

"I'm afraid I need to take my leave, ladies," I announced, tilting my head forward with respect. "It seems that my associate here requires my help with another errand." Catching Mrs. Pickering's gaze, I added, "How long will you still be needing Mrs. St. James?"

It felt odd addressing Catriona that way, but I knew it was a title that removed suspicions. No one needed to know we were far from the typical married couple.

She waved me away impatiently. "You can't rush perfection, Mr. St. James. Go, take care of your business, and return in a few hours. By then I should have most of the measurements needed to create a wardrobe fit for a queen."

To show me just how unimportant my being there was, she then turned her back to me and continued talking with Catriona and her apprentice quietly.

Thoroughly dismissed, I bowed once more and left the house, Knox in tow.

"Good God," he complained once we found ourselves out on the street. "How are you not tearing your hair out from boredom?" Knox threw one last glance over his shoulder before climbing into my coach behind me. "All that material and lace." He shuddered hard.

"It paled in comparison to where I placed my focus," I chuckled, giving him a knowing look. "Heaven help me, but I've grown to appreciate my . . ." It was on the tip of my tongue to call her my wife. Thankfully, I caught myself in time. "My new friend."

Knox snorted, recognizing my explanation as the falsehood it was. He was gracious enough to let me continue fooling myself, anyway.

"I hate to tell you, but I don't think you'll have any better luck talking to her Ladyship's footman. He was quite firm in her refusal." Knox bounced up and down as the carriage wheels hit an uneven portion of the cobblestone road. "I tried every kind of plea to convince him. I even took a page out of your book and offered to throw an obscene amount of money for him to turn a blind eye."

It was a dig at my spending a year's monetary allotment on Catriona's wardrobe.

"And you told them it was a matter of life and death?" I asked, trying to think of any other way to approach the London seer. "That my sanity hangs in the balance?"

"Does it?" Knox fired back, that ridiculous smirk on his face again. He was thoroughly enjoying the way Catriona had gotten under my skin. I hadn't breathed so much as a syllable regarding the change of heart that was currently happening, but somehow, he still knew. It was the consequence of assigning him the very specific role of ensuring that I didn't lose what little humanity I had to the beast that lurked inside. "I would have said your control was slipping the moment you announced Catriona was going to join us today so she could go shopping."

I couldn't deny it. It was definitely a sidestep from my usual behavior. "It seems I need to remind you, again, that I am the master in this relationship, Phineas. Although—" I let out a heavy sigh. "I'm tempted to side with you. Love is a fickle thing that has turned on even the strongest of men and rendered them blithering idiots. Maybe, instead of petitioning Lady Hannah, you should take me to the nearest asylum and have me committed."

I knew the second I closed my mouth that I had revealed the secret I'd been harboring in my heart since I'd woken from our shared dream.

"Love?" Knox was too damn observant for his own good.

"Shut up," I grumbled back. "My feelings aren't a subject for discussion."

I peered out the carriage window at the passing scenery. London was always a bustling town—filled with people going to and from— both the upper and lower classes coexisting. They didn't acknowledge that they all walked the same paths and needed each other to maintain whatever level of lifestyle they enjoyed.

"So, do you really want to try again?" Knox asked, his fingers drumming against his knee as he studied me.

"With Catriona?" I replied absentmindedly.

He burst out laughing. "No, with the sole reason you journeyed to London. You wanted to ask the seer if she could shed any light on the gypsies and where they were hiding." Knox shook his head at me, a look of bewilderment on his face. "Or does that no longer matter?

Maybe I should give up my attempts to break the curse as well. You know . . . now that you've found love."

I banged hard on the roof of the carriage, demanding that the driver stop immediately. I kicked at the door, making it fly open.

"I'll say this once: whatever I may feel for Catriona is not up for discussion or ridicule. Nothing and *no one* will stand in my way, do you understand? My first priority—my *only* priority—will always be to undo that bloody curse and then destroy those who dared harm me. Everything," I thundered passionately, small flecks of spit flying from my lips, "everything I do—that I order you to do—is for that one purpose. All I have is my revenge, Knox. I would caution you to never forget that."

I expected him to argue back, or to at least act indignant that I'd chastised him, but he did neither. He actually grinned wider, and it made me wonder who was the crazier of us two.

"Good to hear that, master," he replied, acting submissive by bowing low. "The apothecary had many of the ingredients I needed for my new experiments. It would be a shame if they went to waste because you've been struck with Cupid's arrow."

And with that, Knox reached over and closed the coach door, signaling the driver to continue on.

"I'm sure you presented my case well, but refusing a servant as opposed to a master and gentleman . . . I would feel much better talking with her footman myself." I relaxed back into the seat and gently smoothed out the creases forming in my trousers. "I can be quite persuasive."

As we jostled toward the seer's Cavendish Square residence, I vowed that I wouldn't leave until I had gained what I wanted.

And should she continue to refuse?

Then I would take what I needed by force.

# CHAPTER 11

The tension in the carriage was practically palpable.

Gone were the plans to spend a few days in London, introducing Catriona to society, and showing her that I could be the reformed "monster" she wanted. While I wasn't promising her sonnets and a showering of hothouse flowers, a night listening to a popular opera singer would have gone a long way toward softening the damage I'd already done.

All plans came to a crashing halt when the front door of Lady Hannah's home slammed shut in my face—denying me entrance to talk with her.

The force I'd threatened to use was extinguished as easily as blowing out a candle. Before Knox could pull me back, I had pushed against the door with my body, determined to rip it from its hinges if needed.

A pulse of explosive magic zapped across my body, sizzling the hair on my arms with its current and almost throwing me off my feet and down the steps onto the street. It made sense that the famous seer had taken the necessary precautions to protect her residence, but it didn't help my wounded pride any.

A crowd quickly gathered at the gate, watching with astonished faces when I repeatedly tried breaking through the spell that now barred my entrance.

It had been a humiliating waste of energy, but that hadn't kept me from my repeated attempts. It wasn't until Knox finally dragged me away, whispering the need for decorum, that I remembered who and where I was. Word would spread like wildfire and make me the brunt of the gossip mill's mockery.

Amidst my cussing and vehement promises to burn the damn town to the ground for this slight, Knox had gotten me back into the carriage. We returned to Mrs. Pickering's seamstress shop without another word spoken and retrieved Catriona. Arrangements were made to have the new clothes delivered to Smithersby Field, and we were gone within the next hour.

Since then, I'd sat fuming in the coach, staring out the window while Knox and Catriona quietly talked to each other. Every now and then I caught a furtive glance from her, but after a while, she gave up trying to ease me into a lighter conversation.

As if to match my mood, a dark storm was rolling in from the east, making it all the more important for us to reach our destination. The roads were treacherous enough without having to navigate around potholes filled with water.

Knox seemed to have the same thought as he studied our surroundings. A crease lined his brow, and for what seemed like the hundredth time, he massaged his temple gingerly with his fingers.

"What?" I barked, noticing that his concern wasn't lifting.

He didn't answer immediately, instead leaning forward to get a better look outside.

"Something doesn't feel right, Marcus," he murmured, loud enough that I caught his response. "I know you'd rather continue traveling until we reach home, but I can't shake the feeling that we would fare better if we traveled during the day, and not during this storm."

I glanced at Catriona to see if she also felt the same. She remained tight-lipped, but her features gave away her similar worry. Her hands fidgeted in her lap, crumpling the material of her dress.

"We should be safe, Knox," I answered, peering forward to where the driver sat, controlling the horses with his leather rein. "If we push the horses, and don't stop as often, we should arrive with no problems. Unless you're truly worried about a mere storm?" I ribbed him, knowing it would gall him to admit his fear.

"Does that look like a mere storm to you?" he countered, challenging me. "It looks as though the gods themselves are angry and have unleashed their wrath on us petty mortals."

I exhaled sharply. "When did you become so dramatic? You sound more like a woman than a man, your delicate sensibilities all aflutter." I raised my voice until it sounded more like Catriona's than mine. I was in no mood to be argued with.

"Damn you," he answered angrily, his gaze narrowing on me. "I would follow you into Hell itself, Marcus, and that may make me a fool, but mark my words—there's an ill wind out tonight, and we need to find shelter."

"Do you agree?" I turned my focus to Catriona. "Do you believe we'll be struck down by lightning if we don't find a place to spend the night?"

She raised her hands in defense, as if she could somehow hold off my frustration and annoyance. "Will you not listen to common sense? If you're not afraid of getting caught in the storm, are you at least aware that the darker it gets, the braver ruffians will be as they see us traveling the road home?" Then with that steel and spitfire nature I'd grown to admire, she threw in another consideration. "Is your pride that important that you would risk your life—our lives? What of your holy mission to bring down the vengeance of heaven against your enemies? You can't do that if you're dead, Marcus. Please, take a deep breath and think."

I slammed my mouth shut—unable to see a way to counter her opinion. She was right, and it rankled me down to my very last nerve.

"She's right, and you know it, master," Knox added, his own sarcasm evident as it dripped from the title he used for me. "You have a right to be angry. What you don't have the right to is taking risks with everyone else's lives."

I let out another drawn-out breath, my fists clenching and unclenching. Before I could change my mind, I caved, and banged on the roof once more. "Driver, stop at the next town so we can find shelter."

"As you wish," came the muffled reply.

"Thank you." Catriona rested her hand lightly on my arm, the warmth of her touch breaching the barriers my clothes provided. "We can start again tomorrow and together," she added, making sure I understood that I wouldn't be alone. "Together we'll find a way to meet with the seer. I promise you that I won't rest until I can help you. Both Knox and I stand with you."

It was her humbled compassion that broke through the bitter fog I'd cloaked myself with, and I finally relaxed. She'd somehow managed to reach deep inside and find the right words to calm me.

"We'll leave at dawn," I grumbled.

"And not a second later," she promised, an enchanting smile tweaking the edges of her mouth.

Knox huffed his disbelief, and he reclined in his own seat, arms crossed over his chest. It would seem his own pride had been pricked with my buckling under the words of Catriona, but he would have to get over it.

With the decision made, and the tension in the carriage slowly dissipating, I closed my eyes, the rocking of the coach lulling me softly into a light sleep.

CATRIONA'S SCREAM filled the air, causing my heart to immediately sink with dread.

The coach had come to a stop only moments ago, and as my eyes flew open, I saw that we were no longer traveling the dusty road alone. Assailants with faces darkened by shadow approached by horseback, their murderous shouts disturbing the peace we'd been enjoying.

Despite my protests to continue on with the hopes of outrunning the attackers, we'd been brought to a halt.

One look was all that was needed between Knox and me. We were no strangers to danger—of protecting ourselves from those with nefarious plans. There was no doubt in my mind that those rapidly surrounding our carriage weren't merely asking for directions.

A sense of foreboding settled over me and with a quick nod—paired with a knowing glance—to Knox, we both flew out of the carriage fully prepared to unleash our fury at being disturbed.

The scent of blood on the air slapped me in the face, and it triggered my throbbing hunger. I didn't always let the darkness that I kept heavily restrained deep inside me free. But the second I caught that familiar coppery scent, mingling with the adrenaline coursing through my veins, I launched myself at the closest assailant to me.

He was no match for the strength I fired at him. As he lay bleeding on the ground, my fangs punched out from my gums, but there would be no time to feed.

I assessed the situation.

Knox was currently trying to hold off three attackers with clubs, his feet kicking out while one of the men struggled to hold him. Rage like I'd never seen from my friend radiated from him, and it was all because two other attackers were dragging a screaming Catriona away from the coach to where their horses stood, waiting.

In the second it took to calculate a response, I ripped off my jacket so the tight item wouldn't hinder my movements. With hands curled up into fists, I threw myself at those beating the hell out of Knox—my hands pounding against soft flesh over and over again.

"Catriona!" Knox bellowed, surging toward her. "Marcus! They mean to take her."

Her kidnappers were almost to their horses when I abandoned helping him and leveled the full weight of my fury toward them. Horses whinnied and reared back as they sensed the beast inside me surge to the surface.

Her look of relief was fleeting when one of the brutes manhandling her released her and came thundering at me—his knife extended, slashing through the air.

"Release her!" I ordered, my voice loud above the ruckus. Its volume rivaled the thunder rumbling in the distance. "This will be your only warning." I swung at the older man with straggly brown hair, mud used to obscure his features and darken his eyes. "You have no idea who you are dealing with."

My fingers grasped tightly on his arm, and I pulled hard, catching him off guard. With hands that now resembled claws, desperate to rip out his throat and gouge the eyes from his head, I let go of whatever humanity I'd managed to safeguard, and fully embraced the monstrous nature that had plagued me all these years.

I didn't hold back.

I had no desire to restrain the demon.

With a ferocity unlike anything I'd ever experienced, I slashed at the man, disarming him easily, but instead of using his knife against him, I bared my teeth—intent on ripping the flesh from his bones myself.

Horror blazed in his eyes, and I reveled in it.

He knew he was facing death. I would personally deliver him to the gates of Hell for ever thinking he could take from me what was mine.

Blood sprayed everywhere as chunks of flesh fell to the ground.

Weakened by the intensity of my counterattack, the man made the sign of the cross, offering a brief prayer to a God I knew would not be listening. As far as I was concerned, he had better chances of survival by petitioning for my mercy, not some invisible deity in the sky.

But I was in no mood to dispense mercy.

As Catriona continued to scream and fight for her freedom, I gave one last kick and slash at the man in front of me and stepped over him as he toppled to the ground—dead.

In a cold, still voice that carried over the melee, I stooped down long enough to retrieve the knife and pointed it at the fool who held my wife.

"Are you next?" I paced toward him, my steely gaze never leaving his stoic features. "Tell me, shall we bury you beside your dead companion?"

I wiped at my face, my fingers coming back wet with blood.

Without thinking, I licked at the ichor, receiving strength from the taste. My response was met with a look of disgust as Catriona's sole kidnapper now grasped her tightly from behind, slowly backing up to his horse.

"I am saving her from you," he growled, spitting on the ground. "I know who—*what* you are."

"Marcus," Catriona begged, desperately trying to break free so she could rush toward me. "They knew we would be traveling tonight. They were waiting."

I took the briefest of seconds to look at her—to really look at the woman who had first been such a hindrance, but had over time worked her way into my heart. I'd been a fool to deny that happiness didn't have to be sacrificed in order to honor my vengeance. All these months, I could've savored our time together, instead of acting like the bastard I'd been.

"I know," she mouthed. That's when it hit me—I may have held her at arm's length, but Catriona had used her time more wisely. She'd quietly been studying the man she'd married, learning to read my body language so she could better understand me. And now—when what she needed was for me to be her hero—I realized that was exactly what I wanted.

Revenge be damned.

She was now the driving force behind my wanting to be a better man, even if that meant living with the curse for the rest of her days.

"Catriona," I roared, and with a strength I hadn't felt since before the alleyway, I stalked toward her, ready to gut the man who restrained her.

My focus zeroed in on him.

All sound seemed to fade around us.

My heart thudded loudly in my ears, my chest trying to adjust to the raggedness of my breathing.

I was death.

I was retribution.

I was a man defending the woman he loved.

"Marcus!" It was Knox who yelled now, from somewhere behind

me. I didn't turn, however, not willing to give the bastard holding Catriona a chance to gain the upper hand. If he reached his horse, he could whisk her away in a heartbeat—each stride taking her farther and farther away.

"I will gut your bitch," the man hissed as he pressed the knife's blade into her stomach. "Like the filthy swine she is."

"Marcus!" she screamed again, her eyes wide as saucers, and with what little energy she had left, Catriona raised her hand, pointing to something behind me.

I didn't think. Later, I would relive this precise moment over and over—my failings repeating in different ways as I agonized over what happened next. Instead, I turned about to see what had caught her attention.

Everything slowed.

Knox was racing toward us, a wild desperation radiating from his features.

In front of him by a few strides came a bulky mammoth of a man with his fist cocked back, aimed at my head.

It was all the distraction they needed.

The giant collided with me, knocking us both to the ground. Knox reached shortly after, and began pulling to get me free.

"Not me, you fool!" I exclaimed. "Protect her!"

But it was too late.

I watched in absolute horror as Catriona was whisked up onto the horse's back, and with a loud crack of the reins, disappeared into the dark surroundings with the gloating ruffian.

A gurgled laughter broke the spell.

"She wasn't yours, *shimulo*." His lips were curled up into a smug smirk. Blood streamed from the open cuts on his head, the scent dancing around me like a siren.

"She is mine!" I thundered, cocking back my fist and striking him with every ounce of strength I possessed. "Where did you take her, gypsy?"

His use of the word had told me exactly who our attackers had been.

"To freedom." He laughed again, and this time spat in my face. "Which is more than you gave my brother Nikolai."

Vengeance.

Why did it always come back to it?

"Marcus, we can still follow. Forget him. Let's go."

For as long as I lived, I would never forget the expression the gypsy wore as I used his body to gain my balance and stand. It was a mix of ruthlessness and gloating satisfaction. In his mind, we would never reach them in time to stop whatever plans they had for Catriona.

"Give my regards to the Devil," I sneered, bending over one last time. "Make sure he knows that your clan will be joining you shortly." And with one violent swipe of my clawed hand, I tore at his throat, exposing his jugular to the air. Blood gushed out, and within moments, he was dead.

"Hurry," Knox urged, having retrieved two horses that had somehow remained despite the melee.

Swinging up into the saddle, I left everything behind and galloped into the darkness, uttering yet another promise I fully intended to honor.

"If she dies, they all die."

# CHAPTER 12

The scent of blood and carnage hung in the air.

Wiping my hands down the sides of my pant legs, I surveyed the damage Knox and I had delivered.

The justice we had served.

All around us, battered bodies lay where they had fallen—an entire gypsy clan wiped out. Nowhere did I feel an inkling of remorse. They'd brought this destruction down upon their own heads when they dared kidnap Catriona, attacking us as we traveled home.

This was the price of the war we waged—both parties hoping to deal out vengeance.

Nikolai had been one of their kinsfolk, and I'd made sure that his wife and child knew that he'd died quickly by my hand. Had the clan released Catriona into my care, I may have shown them some kind of benevolence and spared at least the children.

But as Knox tore apart their camp site, rifling through caravans and tents, there was no hint that she'd even arrived. When she didn't respond to our calls—no sign of the beautiful woman who'd changed my entire world for the better—a cold seething began building inside me where all I could see was red.

Knox knew better than to warn me against unleashing the storm that still boiled within my veins. When I had the leader down on his knees—begging for the lives of his family—there was no room for negotiating. Tears fell from his eyes as I vowed to wipe out his lineage before slitting his throat.

I had rained down death with no qualms or hesitancy.

One brave fool had stepped forward with the derisive taunt that Catriona would be defiled and murdered before I could ever hope to reach her. That this vile act was to repay the anguish I'd inflicted by killing their beloved Nikolai.

Over and over, clan members tried bargaining for the lives of others—offering hollow promises that they could somehow produce Catriona, whole and unharmed.

But I saw their words as the lies they were.

From my experience, twisted as it may be, gypsies were a ruthless, amoral group of people that deserved the wrath I was about to rain down on them.

And I had.

Side by side with Knox, we had systematically erased the entire group from existence, tossing their soulless bodies to the side as we made sure there were no survivors.

"She isn't here," Knox cried, his voice thick with emotion. He had loved her too—he was her protector from me when I had failed to see her for what she was.

A treasure to be cherished.

A woman who had somehow managed to tame the beast.

"Then we will hunt her kidnappers to the ends of the earth until we find her." I lashed out to the pot of food hanging over the fire someone had lit. The fragrant stew splashed across the ground, flecks of gravy splattering the lifeless body of the woman responsible for it. "They will all pay for this!"

I stood there, shaking my fists at the sky, and all the bitterness I'd felt over the past decade came flooding back until all I could feel was the vampire nature I'd been cursed with.

Marcus the man had been obliterated, and I didn't mourn the death of him.

I'd lowered my guard, allowing the light to touch those parts of me, and for what? So someone could come crashing in and steal what was most precious to me—again.

Knox's hand fell hard on my shoulder, his fingers squeezing in an attempt to comfort. I shrugged him away. There would be no more solace or peace.

"She was mine to protect," I uttered, slowly regaining my breath. Adrenaline still coursed through my veins, and the bloodlust still stoked my anger. "She was mine, and they took her."

"We can still catch them," Knox stated, convinced the odds were still in our favor. He was covered in blood, and judging from the red patch at his side, he was also injured. When I pushed my fingers against the material, he winced.

There was no hiding it.

"You're in no condition to ride. I will go. You'll only slow me down." My foot caught on something, and I looked down to find my boot had snagged a small doll made from rough material—the toy still in the tight grasp of a child.

I couldn't think about the ramifications, of the people I'd made victims by my rage tonight. Any chink in the armor I now wore would weaken my resolve. Right now, I had one mission . . . one focus. Catriona was still out there, and by all that was holy, I *would* be her knight in shining armor.

"You need me," Knox gasped, pain hitting him again, and his stance faltered, his knees threatening to give out under him. "Just get me on my horse."

I shook my head. "I can't wait for you, Phineas. Every second we waste here is another second they have her."

He tried to stop me from walking away, but his own blood loss made him drop to his knees finally. Frustrated that he was now useless, Knox pounded his fist on the ground. A flurry of words coated with resentment and outrage burst from his lips. He was angry—justifiably.

"I will bring back her kidnapper. He will be yours to administer justice to. You have my word." I extended my arm quickly, clasping his in a warrior-like handshake, slowly pulling him to his feet. "Ride for home. Seek medical help at the next town." Consumed with a sudden feeling of family, I grabbed him at the back of the head, pressing our foreheads together. "Live for me, my brother. Live for her."

"Go," he ushered, waving me on. "Go with God."

As I swung my leg up and over my new ride, I let out a cynical laugh. "I don't know about God, but I would be grateful for any kind of divine assistance tonight."

With one last look as my horse turned in a circle impatiently, I kicked in my heels and spurred the beast onward.

My new enemy had a head start, but I had one thing aiding me that he'd underestimated.

I would never rest until I found her.

I would never rest until I held her safely in my arms.

# CHAPTER 13

## ONE WEEK LATER

*M*y heart hurt.

As in it physically hurt me to arrive home empty-handed.

Despite my most valiant efforts, the one who'd taken my Catriona had disappeared like a thief in the night, and all my attempts at tracking him had failed.

I'd been so cocky and sure that I would find them. Each hour that passed fueled the fantasies I created, where I punished the fool for his audacity in stealing her. She truly was an innocent in all of this—and they'd chosen their target well when he'd taken off with her.

Kill me, and it would end this pitiful existence I endured.

Kill Knox, and it would slow down the search for a cure, but ultimately, he was replaceable. I didn't like that thought, because Phineas had become more like a brother to me. It wasn't something I ever acknowledged, but all my beliefs and opinions had been blasted to smithereens now that I'd lost everything.

But to touch her, to defile her virtue, to sully her very body—that was unforgivable.

No matter how hard I rode, or the many villages and towns I stopped at, the results were the same.

No one had seen her or the villain who had stolen her. There were no leads. No witnesses came forward, despite the generous reward I offered for information. I didn't care how insignificant the news was, either. I was prepared to pay handsomely for a mere glimpse of her.

It had rendered me a desperate man, and that irritated me. What was needed now was force and ruthlessness. Instead, I acted like a panicked, lovesick male who'd lost his mind over a woman.

On and on I rode, chasing shadows until I had to finally admit defeat. I was tired. I was hungry. I had to return to feeding on stragglers late at night as they stumbled home from the local tavern. My impatience made me brutal—my thirst demanding its fill.

Yet, here I was again at Smithersby Field, alone.

Stabling the horse and leaving instructions with the boy I'd hired to care for the beasts, I headed toward the house, but found myself lured to the private glen in the woods.

The headstone seemed to glow beneath the moonlight, an eerie beckoning from the ghost that still haunted me.

Primrose.

It had all begun with her, and now another grave would be dug to hold my beloved Catriona.

It would be a testament to the two women I had failed terribly.

Sinking onto the bench, I buried my face in my hands and wept. Hot tears streaked down my cheeks, clinging for a moment under my chin before falling to the ground. I didn't bother hiding the raw emotion consuming me.

I felt it—all of it.

"Marcus?"

The sound of my name made me jump with surprise. I hadn't heard anyone approach, and while my soul rejoiced in hearing Knox speak, it couldn't extinguish the sorrow that filled me.

My sobs grew louder, and as he wrapped his arms around my shoulder, I let go and fully gave in to my grief.

"I couldn't find her." My words came out in ragged breaths, my chest heaving. "I searched. I begged. I threatened, and it was all in vain. I failed her, and by not bringing her home, I have failed you, too."

He didn't speak, allowing me to purge the twisted feelings that had been buried inside me for so long. I didn't bother wiping away my tears. There was no need for masculine pride. When I finally looked up, I instantly saw I wasn't the only one who was caught up in misery.

His expression was one of absolute solemnness. He knew what it meant for me to bare my soul to him, to expose myself so completely that it would forever change our friendship.

We were no longer master and servant.

We weren't really friends and comrades either.

We were family.

We were brothers.

All we had seen and experienced had forged an unbreakable bond, and as we fell back into silence, we mourned our loss together.

Eventually the cool air became impossible to ignore, and wiping my face, I let out an exhausted sigh.

"What have I missed in my absence?" Despite what had happened, the estate still required my attention. I hated it, but honoring my responsibilities would give me an outlet until I devised a new plan.

Catriona may very well be dead.

I would add her name to my list of grievances.

Knox reached into his coat and pulled out a sealed letter, handing it to me. "This came a few days ago with the strictest of commands that only you could open and read it."

"Do you know who it's from?" I asked, turning over the folded paper and lightly tracing the waxed seal keeping it together. The insignia wasn't familiar, but that didn't mean anything. Perhaps it was a petition from the nearby town for aid to make it through the winter. As one of the big houses and estates in the area, people often looked to me for help during the tough season.

I often refused them, or sent them meager supplies, but for Catriona, I would grant whatever they requested. She had changed me. I refused to dishonor her memory.

Cracking the wax, I slowly unfolded the letter, and started reading.

"What does it say?" Knox asked, peering over my shoulder. "Who is it from?"

I couldn't answer as a lump formed in my throat, hope flaring within my chest. The second I finished the short message, I read it again . . . and again. Over and over as if it would somehow explain itself.

When I couldn't keep quiet any longer, I crumpled the message in my hand and stood—a new excitement sweeping away my despair.

There was an emotion at the forefront, one I'd assumed I'd never feel again.

Hope.

"Come, we need to pack. I want to be gone within the hour." I didn't offer any other explanation, and to Knox's credit, he acted immediately, following me back to the house.

We each retreated to our bedchambers, throwing clothes into trunks before meeting at the bottom of the grand staircase. I'd already left instructions with the hired help that would stay behind. Even though the message wasn't from the town, I'd still asked that food from the storehouse be taken to the people there.

"Are you really going to keep me in the dark, Marcus? Where are we going?" Knox threw me an impatient look that warned me should I not include him in the mystery, he would take the letter and read it himself. Forcibly, if needed.

I didn't answer. I offered him the letter that I'd placed in my pocket.

His lips moved as he silently mouthed the few words contained in the message. Nodding, he met my gaze.

We were united.

We had purpose.

We had a lead.

"Let's go," I said. Without a second thought, I walked through the door, unsure whether I'd ever return to my ancestral home, but not caring.

I didn't know what dangers we might face. The future was as

murky as ever, but for the small flicker of hope that now burned within my heart.

I was blood and damnation.

I would finally lay claim to what was mine.

I would become wrath and retribution.

I was Marcus St. James, and in my pocket, I held the key to the answers I was seeking.

# EPILOGUE

## ONE YEAR LATER, 1879

*W*ith dust-covered clothes, we arrived at the designated place. I still wasn't sure why there was a need for all the secrecy, but after traveling this far, there was no way I would be turned from my goals.

Lady Hannah's note may have been short, but I chose to see it as certainty. This was where she said I would find the answers I was seeking. She was a celebrated seer—someone who was well known within the supernatural community for her accuracy. I'd asked, and she'd responded by using her gifts of foresight.

Glancing about, I was shocked to see that this was where our journey had ended. The rugged wildness of Colorado was breathtaking, and so different from the world I'd left behind in England. I could see why so many were flocking to the Americas—in particular to the land they now called the United States of America. People came in search of freedom, of finding their fortune, of changing the circumstances of their upbringing. The beauty that surrounded Knox and me right now, with majestic mountains and greenery—the fresh air a testament that it remained untouched by civilization—I could see myself joining the others in staking my claim here.

Perhaps if this lead failed to provide the answers I was seeking, Knox and I could remain and see where a new life might take us. No one would know us here. No one would know me. It could be a fresh start for a monster like me.

"Are you sure this is where we were to meet our contact?" Knox murmured, scanning the area, looking to see if anyone approached.

I nodded, remembering the conversation we'd last had at the town miles away. After a week of asking around, of trying to find anyone who knew about the town Lady Hannah had named on the paper she'd sent, we'd almost given up and moved on.

Why would she send us on a wild goose chase across the ocean to a place that people had never heard about? Did such a town even exist?

Finally, after we finished our evening meal, a stranger approached us in the saloon where we were staying, discreetly asking us to follow him outside. Once we were out in the alleyway, he'd asked us about our queries, not once giving away whether he held the answers we needed or not.

If anything, the idea of being there in that alleyway—another one in another time and place—had given me the sense of coming full circle. Knox felt the same wariness, never once taking his hand off the concealed knife that he had strapped to his thigh. Desperation wasn't an excuse to lower our guards. We hadn't come this far to meet our end in the Colorado mountains.

The stranger had listened, and then with a sweeping look, told us to await further instructions. Sure enough, early this morning, I found a note slid under the door of our room with the directions for a secret meeting.

"We've come this far. Let's see what happens next," I replied, licking my lips nervously. There was a weariness about Knox, his expression tired from the constant traveling. I was grateful for his company, happy that he was standing here beside me.

There was a crunching sound that told us immediately that we weren't alone.

"Be on guard," I uttered beneath my breath. Knox touched the side of his leg, where the large knife was. I readied myself in case this was an ambush. If there was one thing I'd learned from my experiences with the gypsies I'd met, it was that it was deadly to walk into a situation unprepared.

"There will be no need for violence," a deep voice spoke. A second later, a tall man appeared—one whose demeanor screamed authority. Whoever he was, he was a leader. "I called for this meeting so we could talk, not fight."

I assessed him quickly—was he friend or foe?

He was neatly dressed with his dark hair slicked back. There was a small scar under his left eye—which was the darkest blue I'd ever seen. Sizing him up, I stepped toward him.

"My name is Marcus St. James, and this is my companion, Phineas Knox." We both bowed our heads with respect, hoping that it would work in our favor.

I wasn't the only one sizing people up. He gave me another once over and nodded. "My name is Roman Bishop. I understand you've been asking questions about my town." There was a strong sense of pride as he spoke. "I hope you understand that I'm protective of the people I lead. I can't let just anyone into our home."

He definitely gave off a no-nonsense attitude. I knew it would work against us if I was completely honest and told him I was here on a mission of revenge. Half-truths would have to be enough for right now.

Wetting my lips, I answered. "I can respect that, Roman Bishop. I feel the same about my own kin; in fact, that's what's brought us here. My wife was kidnapped over a year ago, and our search has led us here, to your town."

I watched him as I spoke, trying to gauge his response. I caught the flicker of anger at the mention of Catriona being kidnapped and the furrowing of his brow. It gave me hope.

Knox chose to speak up next. "We're not here to cause any trouble. We've experienced enough during our travels. All we want is to find her so we can return home to England." The earnestness in his tone was convincing.

Roman Bishop looked back and forth between us. "There are rules you will need to follow should you be allowed to enter my town. Do you agree to abide by the law?"

We both nodded. I knew I wasn't the only one curious about the town now. "You have my word as a gentleman."

I extended my hand in agreement and with only a slight hesitation, Roman shook it. His handshake was strong and firm.

"Then welcome to Havenwood Falls, gentlemen. May you find the answers you seek."

We hope you enjoyed this story in the Legends of Havenwood Falls series featuring a variety of supernatural creatures. The series is a collaborative effort by multiple authors.

Books by Belinda Boring in the Havenwood Falls world:
*Nowhere to Hide*
*The Collector: Awakening*
*Addicted to You*
*Blood and Damnation*
*Wrath and Retribution*
*Sun & Moon Academy Book One: Fall Semester*
*Sun & Moon Academy Book Two: Spring Semester*

Books in the historical Legends of Havenwood Falls series:

*Lost in Time* by Tish Thawer
*Dawn of the Witch Hunters* by Morgan Wylie
*Redemption's End* by Eric R. Asher
*Trapped Within a Wish* by Brynn Myers
*Blood and Damnation* by Belinda Boring
*Fated Beginnings* by E.J. Fechenda
*Emeline* by Katie M. John
*Released From a Curse* by Brynn Myers
*A Pack of Lies* by Kallie Ross

*Kiss the Ashes* by Desiree Lafawn
*Hidden Truths* by Colleen Nye
*Wrath and Retribution* by Belinda Boring
*Changing Fate* by Char Webster
*Rise of the Witch Hunters* by Morgan Wylie
*The Drowning Bride* by Seven Jane

Also try the main Havenwood Falls series; the YA line, Havenwood Falls High; the darker, sexier side of town, Havenwood Falls Sin & Silk; and the local supernatural college, Sun & Moon Academy.

Stay up to date at www.HavenwoodFalls.com

Subscribe to our reader group and receive free stories and more!

# ABOUT THE AUTHOR

International and #1 Multi-Genre Bestselling Author Belinda Boring is known to many readers as the Queen of Swoon and also the Queen of Cliffhangers. Her Mystic Wolves series has topped many charts, along with receiving several awards and nominations such as Paranormal Book of the Year, Best Debut Book, as well as being in the Top 3 Best Rated on Amazon. With additional titles like Wanderlust, Enchanted Hearts, Loving Liberty and Broken Promises, it's easy to see why readers are captivated by this swoon-worthy author!

A homesick Aussie living amongst the cactus and mountains of Arizona, Belinda Boring is a self-proclaimed addict of romance and all things swoon-worthy. It wasn't long before she began writing, pouring her imagination and creativity into the stories she dreams. Whether urban fantasy, paranormal romance or romance in general, Belinda strives to share great plots with heart and characters that you can't help but connect with. Of course, she wouldn't be Belinda without adding heroes she hopes will curl your toes. Surrounded by a supportive cast of family, friends, and the man she gives her heart and soul to, Belinda is living the good life.

# ACKNOWLEDGMENTS

I fell in love with Marcus St. James immediately. From the moment he stepped forward in my mind, I knew he had a story that would reach in and claim my heart. He's not the typical hero. He's a jerk, and there were times were I had to pause, cock my own eyebrow, and say, "Really? You're going to be THAT kind of guy?" But what can I say? I love the broken hero, the reluctant hero, the hero who thinks he has it all figured out, only to realize he is CLUELESS. I hope you fall for him like I did. I hope that you can see his heart . . . it's there, I promise. I like to believe that the harder someone falls, the greater their redemption is. He's worth it—they all are!

I wanted to thank everyone behind the scenes who helped bring this story to fruition:

My husband and family, who are always so supportive and patient while I'm writing. I sometimes wish that brainstorming came with a frequent driving card or something because Mark and I totally racked up the miles driving about our small town. #LostWithoutYou

My beta readers who faithfully read each chapter and gave amazing feedback. You guys are invaluable to me so *lick* you're mine FOREVER! Thank you for always being there and begging for more. Your comments made me chuckle! #StuckWithMe

My author coach, Jessica Gibson, who cracks that whip of hers with expertise! Thank you for keeping me focused and motivated, especially when I have a tendency to squirrel over a bazillion things OTHER than what I'm meant to be writing. Thanks for always being in my corner. #BabeBossForever

Lastly, I wanted to thank Kristie Cook and all my fellow

Havenwood Falls authors, for being part of my journey. I LOVE Havenwood Falls. I LOVE the stories that have been shared and what each of you bring to this incredible world. Thank you for welcoming me with open arms and being part of my book world family. I'm proud to stand amongst you and call you all friends! #SappyBels

For those who love author insights, I wrote this entire story to one song: It's Quiet Uptown by Lin-Manuel Miranda. I'm obsessed with all things Hamilton and when it came time to build this story's playlist, this was the ONLY song I could write to. It sets the tone beautifully so, please, if you're curious, have a listen to the music and see if it helps capture your heart.

Happy reading, everyone! Thanks for visiting Havenwood Falls with me. 🤍

Belinda

xoxo

A Legends of Havenwood Falls Novella

# HAVENWOOD FALLS

## LEGENDS

## FATED
# BEGINNINGS

# E.J. FECHENDA

## *Fated Beginnings* (A Legends of Havenwood Falls Novella) by E.J. Fechenda

Ever since he was a young boy, Daniel McCabe and his family have been running to escape his father's past—a past scarred by the cruelty of humans against their kind. Indian reservations, the Japanese internment camps of World War II, and racial segregation only reinforce what he's been taught: humans mistreat those who are different. Fearing the same treatment if his shifter abilities are ever discovered, he keeps to himself and trusts very few. While the war may be over, the 1950s seem to be a time of conformity, and Daniel is anything but a conformist.

After Daniel moves his mom back to Colorado, the only place he has really considered home, a job opportunity brings him to a small town nestled in the Rocky Mountains. Havenwood Falls offers the promise of a new beginning—a chance to help the town grow and to establish a life for himself and for others like him. He even finds his mate.

Colleen Campbell is smart, funny, bold, and beautiful. And human.

Havenwood Falls has everything Daniel has dreamt about, offering a stable future with a woman he could love. But if he can't overcome everything he knows and believes, this fated beginning may already be at its end.

# FATED BEGINNINGS

## AN EXCERPT

### SUNSET CREEK, COLORADO AUGUST 1947

Dust billowed out behind the truck, and the dirt road had grown increasingly bumpier and narrower the higher Daniel McCabe's dad drove up the mountain. The truck bounced over ruts and rocks, causing Daniel to bounce in his seat. The last sign of civilization he recalled seeing was a homestead with two sickly looking horses in the corral, emaciated to the point he could count the ribs. He had wanted to stop and give them his apple that was packed with his lunch, but his dad refused. He said there wasn't time to dillydally. He wanted to get to their destination before noon.

Judging by the sun high overhead, that time quickly approached. They passed a sign for Prospector Gulch, and Daniel noticed his dad's grip on the steering wheel tighten, as did the set of his jaw. Sheer determination pushed him forward on this task. When his dad asked him if he wanted to visit Sunset Creek, Daniel didn't hesitate to say yes. Sunset Creek had only been spoken about in whispers, accompanied by expressions of sadness. Daniel knew something bad had happened that had resulted in his grandfather dying, but he didn't know what. Now that they were approaching the old mining town, the place of his father's birth and his grandfather's death, hopefully he'd learn the whole story.

They rounded a bend in the road, and his dad slammed on the brakes, sliding to a stop on the dirt. An aspen tree lay on its side, blocking the way.

"Well," his dad said with a sigh, "looks like we're walking the rest of the way." He grabbed the satchel that contained their lunches and canteens of water before opening the door. Daniel scrambled out after him, eager to stretch his legs. They had been driving all morning. Sunset Creek was located in the mountains in Gunnison National Forest, about two hours west of where they lived in Colorado Springs. Daniel's dad was quiet as they marched along the narrow road so choked with overgrowth, it was hard to believe it was a road at all.

"Dad, how can anyone live out here?"

"Nobody does . . . anymore."

"Why?"

His dad paused and fished out a canteen from the bag. He screwed off the top, took a few deep gulps, and handed it over to Daniel. That's when he noticed his dad's hand was shaking. His dad didn't respond, just turned around and kept walking. Daniel easily kept up. Since he had turned fifteen three months ago, he had gone through a growth spurt. Now his long strides matched his dad's. The forest grew thicker around them, and it was so much quieter out here than in the city. Daniel itched to roam through the woods and smell everything. He was getting better at controlling his shift, and out here, where they hadn't seen any humans and he didn't detect any with his enhanced senses, the urge to be one with nature became increasingly difficult to contain.

As if sensing this, his dad grabbed his wrist. "Not yet," he said. "There will be time later."

Daniel let out a small growl, but nodded in understanding.

"I used to know these woods—they were like my second home once. Before . . ." His dad trailed off, staring off into the distance, but Daniel could tell he was lost in his thoughts. His forehead crinkled before he shook out of his trance and started moving again.

They walked side by side in silence until they reached an old wooden post. On the ground in front of it was a sign. The wood was half rotted, and the white paint faded to the point where some of the letters were gone, but he could still make out the words: Sunset Creek est. 1867. That was eighty years ago, he thought to himself as he took in what was left of the town laid out before him. There were structures left—a few homes and stores—but no sign of life. He could see where the mines had been carved out of the hillside above the town. Rusty machinery dotted the stripped earth. As they walked down the main street through the center of town, Daniel shivered as if ghosts followed them. Looking over at his dad, he could tell he was haunted by memories. Shells of buildings remained. Some of them were half burnt and leaning at a dangerous angle.

"Dad?" His voice shook with fear. "What happened here?"

"Humans. Humans happened." His dad's shoulders slumped as if exhausted, and he focused his blue eyes just past Daniel's shoulders. "Come, it's time you know. You're old enough."

He led them to the front steps of what was once the general store. The windows were busted out, glass littered the front porch, and the wooden door swung in the gentle breeze, rusty hinges letting out an occasional squeak. Once they were settled on the steps with sandwiches that his mom made in their hands, his dad started talking.

"Sunset Creek was a booming mining town in its heyday. The vein of gold they discovered made a lot of men rich. My father—your grandfather, Ian McCabe—arrived here from Ireland in 1875 with his oldest brother, Robert. Robert was seventeen at the time, and my father only thirteen. Even though it was a few years after the vein was first discovered, there was still plenty gold left for him to acquire some wealth.

"In 1878, Sunset Creek was still thriving. Even though the gold vein had been depleted, one of the largest silver veins had been discovered, attracting prospectors like bees to honey.

"As Sunset Creek grew, the boundaries encroached upon unclaimed land where wildlife was plentiful. Hunting and fishing provided a much-needed food source. According to what my father told me, in 1878, William Jenkins, a Sunset Creek resident, had gone out hunting with his twelve-year-old son, Johnny. He returned on the second day without any fresh kills. Instead, the bloody body he carried in his arms was his son. Johnny had been mauled by a mountain lion. William had shot the beast before it could snap his son's neck. A priest was brought in, and last rites were read at Johnny's bedside as he fought for his life. William and Judith Jenkins kept a vigil through the night. Fortunately, he survived, but there were more attacks by mountain lions. Your grandfather was one of the victims."

"What?"

"That's how he became a shifter. He was bitten. Imagine the shock and surprise when he first shifted."

"Holy Toledo!" Daniel sat back in awe. He'd always assumed his grandda was born a shifter like everyone else in his immediate family.

"The mountain lion attacks continued for several years, and multiple residents were bitten. Only after Johnny Jenkins shifted in public during an argument with his father, in front of the assayer's office, did your grandda figure out there were more mountain lion shifters like him. The reaction to Johnny's public change also made him realize he needed to be very careful about who knew his true nature."

"Why?" Daniel asked, leaning forward with his arms propped on top of his knees.

His dad sighed and ran a hand over his beard, which was a deep reddish brown that had only recently become threaded with some white hairs.

"Humans are easily afraid and easily suspicious of anyone they consider different. I mean, you've seen the reservations and the internment camps."

Daniel understood what he was saying. Even though the Second World War had ended two years earlier, pictures of Holocaust survivors that ran in newspapers were burned into his memory. Here in Colorado, the Japanese Internment camps, which the governor fought against, still existed. They were empty, the prisoners released to go back to their lives, but the structures remained as a reminder of how quickly people could turn against a whole group considered different or a threat.

"According to your grandda, it was late one night when a group of men who worked at the mines formed a mob. They had been drinking at the saloon and got riled up. Somebody mentioned Johnny Jenkins, and it escalated from there. They left the bar and marched down Main Street to the Jenkins house."

Daniel's dad paused and stared off across the street at the shell of what used to be the bar. A faded sign that read Silver Spur Saloon had come loose on one end and hung at an angle, partially blocking the doorless entrance. He swallowed once before continuing. "They burnt the fucking house down. Johnny and his family barely escaped."

Daniel's eyes widened, and his mouth hung open in shock, partly because of how horrible the story was, and also because his dad swore. He rarely said cuss words in front of him.

"Apparently, Johnny and his family left that night, and were never seen or heard from again, but things were different after that. Anyone who had been associated with them were cast under suspicion as well. My father kept hoping that things would settle down, but seeing a person transform into a wild animal is something people don't easily forget."

"But he stayed. I mean, you were born here. Why didn't he leave?"

He snorted, and his mouth twisted up in a smile. "Us McCabes are a stubborn lot," he said and winked at Daniel, who returned his grin. "He and his brother had settled in Sunset Creek and that's all they knew. They refused to leave. Also, I think love had something to do with it."

"Oh," Daniel responded with a knowing tone. "Gran."

"Yup. He met my mother, and she didn't have any desire to leave either."

Daniel scratched his head and swatted at a fly buzzing around his ear. The sun had shifted, and he was baking in its full afternoon heat. "Was Gran already a shifter when they met?"

"Yes. She had been bitten, too. As you are learning, we have enhanced senses, so it's easier to pick out nonhumans in a crowd. Soon the mountain lion shifters of Sunset Creek were holding their own gatherings in secret. These gatherings were the only way of exploring the animal side; they were a safe place."

Once again, his dad grew quiet and stared off into the distance. Daniel noticed his eyes shone with tears that never spilled. His dad cleared his throat and stood up. He paced in front of the steps where Daniel sat.

"When I was ten years old, I was with your grandda and gran and my sister at one of these gatherings. Now, mind you, the mines were almost depleted by this time and the population was growing smaller each month as people had to find work elsewhere. This also meant there were a lot of desperate people around. Desperate and angry people are like powder kegs waiting to go off. We thought our gatherings had gone unnoticed, but in a small town, it's hard to keep secrets. Unfortunately, someone noticed, and that was enough to light the fuse."

"What happened?" Daniel was leaning forward by now, completely engrossed in the story. He was finally going to learn what his dad and gran kept secret.

"They came for us. Tried to slaughter us all and came really close to succeeding." His dad's voice was rough with emotion, and he stopped pacing. With a sigh, he sunk down on the steps next to him. His shoulders were hunched over like he was physically burdened by the memory. "Homes were torched, friends were shot in the street . . . it was swift and brutal. I don't know how many survived. We scattered. My dad managed to get us to safety, urged us to head for the nearest town, and said that he'd catch up to us. He went back to fight, and we never saw him again."

Daniel shuddered as he absorbed the information. He had no idea his family history would be so dark. "Did you try to find him?" he asked.

"I wanted to go back and look for him, but your gran insisted we stay far away. She scoured newspapers for any coverage of the violence, but nothing was ever published. She thinks the government covered it up. It's possible. Just look at what's happening in New Mexico. That fellow found a spaceship on his farm, and now the news is saying it's a weather balloon. They probably are testing on aliens right now in some underground bunker. Hell, they probably captured a shifter or two and are testing them, too. All I know is Sunset Creek has been wiped from the map and was left to sink back into the earth. Humans can't be trusted, Daniel. Remember that. They can't handle anything out of the ordinary."

His dad's warnings were nothing new. Daniel had been hearing them his whole life, even more since his first shift, which took place three months ago, not too long after he turned fifteen. Now, knowing the history, he understood why.

He took his dad's warning to heart that day, adapting it as a rule that would follow him into adulthood: be careful who you trust, especially humans.

"I needed to tell you the history, Daniel. It's why we move so much. We can't afford to get too comfortable in one place. Your mother and I know it's been difficult, especially with you getting older."

The images Daniel's imagination conjured up flashed vividly through his mind, the carnage worse than any war movie playing at the local cinema. He pictured streets running red with blood and the empty street before him a scene of total chaos as shifters were slaughtered. His dad was right—he hated moving all the time. Just when he started to settle in and make friends, his family would pick up and move on. It had gotten to the point where he didn't bother making friends.

"Are we moving again?" Daniel asked, hoping to disguise the disappointment in his voice. His dad's expression said it all, in the tight set of his jaw and slight frown.

"I'm afraid so, son. This time we're heading east. West Virginia, to be exact."

Daniel's shoulders dropped, and he hunched over, curling inward and turning his head so his dad didn't see the tears welling in his eyes. It was worse than he could have imagined. Not only were they moving again, but they were leaving Colorado, the only constant—the only state he had always been able to call home.

Two weeks later, they left, Daniel crammed in the cab of the truck next to his mom, who sat in the middle. The truck's bed was piled high with their belongings, covered by a large black tarp to protect their things from rain.

The farther they drove, the more uneasy Daniel grew. He wanted to go back, felt it in his bones that they were heading in the wrong direction, but he was powerless to do anything, forced to follow his parents.

As they crossed the state line and entered Kansas, Daniel made a promise to himself: he would come back. As soon as he was able, he'd make his way back to Colorado.

Purchase *Fated Beginnings* where books are sold.